Don't Call me Baby

Don't Call me Baby

GWENDOLYN HEASLEY

HARPER TEEN
An Imprint of HarperCollinsPublishers

HarperTeen is an imprint of HarperCollins Publishers.

Library of Congress Control Number: 2013956490
ISBN 978-0-06-220852-1 (pbk.)

Typography by Alison Klapthor
14 15 16 17 18   CG/RRDH   10 9 8 7 6 5 4 3 2 1
❖
First Edition

For Cory

Prologue

DO YOU KNOW WHAT IT'S LIKE TO BE RECOGNIZED AT THE MALL by random moms pushing strollers when you're just trying to hang out with your friends?

Do you know what it's like to have strangers at Starbucks say, "Ohmigosh, I've watched you grow up. I'm so glad that your braces finally corrected that awful overbite!"

Do you know what it's like to have your classmates read about you getting your first period?

Do you know what it's like to have everyone think that they know you because of what they read on some stupid website?

I didn't think so. I imagine that Suri Cruise could empathize with me, but at least she has awesome clothes and *actually* famous parents. I'm recognizable because my mother writes a lame, but very popular, blog.

My mom has been a blogger since before I was born. It started out as a healthy-living blog, but then she found out she was pregnant. Ever since then, it's been a mommy blog. (Technically, it was a womb blog for my first nine months.) The thing is, I'm fifteen now, and she's *still* blogging about me. I have two lives: my life as the blogging world knows it and my actual life. You can read my life as my mom tells it on MommyliciousMeg.com. This version is my actual life. Thanks for reading.

Mommylicious

"Back to School"

Imogene is starting the ninth grade today! Can you believe she's fifteen?

Do you remember when she was born? If you don't, click <u>HERE</u>. Do you remember when she first walked? If you don't, click <u>HERE</u>. The first day of pre-school. The first day of middle school. And now, the first day of ninth grade.

(Insert the Niagara Falls of tears over my little girl growing up.)

Even though she's *my* baby, I know that many of you have grown up with her too! After all, y'all named her in that genius contest, and it turns out that she is *such* an Imogene! I have *the* smartest readers.

What does ninth grade mean for Imogene? It's a big one, since it's the last year of uniforms AND the last year before high school. Soon, she'll be driving, and then before we know it, she'll be off to college. But the REALLY huge event in ninth grade is the Halloween Pirate's Booty Ball, which will be Imogene's first date dance.

While listening (okay, maybe I was technically

eavesdropping), I overheard Imogene and a friend *already* talking about who they want to ask them. No spoiler alerts here! I'm just scared that she (or someone else) might get their feelings hurt. What do y'all think: Should there be formal date dances before high school even starts? Send me your feedback!

I can't wait to share Imogene's back-to-school photos tomorrow! I know you guys don't want to miss seeing how grown-up she looks. She's even wearing a real bra these days. You know, the type with underwire and a little padding . . . but shush, don't tell. Where did our baby go?

Butterfly kisses,
Mommylicious!

Chapter One

THE GREAT ESCAPE

CLICK.

I recognize the precise sound of my mom's camera shutter opening and closing.

Instinctively, I dive for cover and throw my pink-and-white seahorse-print Lilly Pulitzer duvet over my head.

"Are you serious, Mom? This can't be happening." I moan, but the goose feathers in the duvet muffle my cries.

"Gotcha!" my mom exclaims. "That was a hilarious shot. And, Imogene, I do befores and afters *every* first day of school. They're *adorable*. Readers love seeing you waking up to a new year. It signals fresh starts for them, too. You *know* this, Imogene."

Just because I know it, doesn't mean I'm okay with it. And I want a reset button just as much as my mom's

5

readers do, one where I'm not the subject/star of a mommy blog.

I stay under my tent of privacy until I'm positive that my mom's exited my room. There's no way I'm going back to sleep for an extra ten minutes when I'm this angry, so I fumble my way into my bathroom for a shower.

I miss summer *already*, and it's not even seven a.m. on the first day of school. As I soap up, I practice the abbreviated version of my "Can this year please be different?" speech.

"Mom," I say to my Bubble & Bee organic shampoo bottle. "We need to talk. I'm in ninth grade now, which means I'm almost in high school, and I don't want to be on your blog every day. I don't *want* people to know what we did over the weekend. I don't want to review clothes or products for your sponsors. I want a normal life where I have privacy. I want to be Imogene, not Babylicious. I want you to be my mom, not Mommylicious."

Even before the conditioner's all the way rinsed out of my hair, I already know that I don't have the guts to give that speech to my mom today. It wouldn't change anything, anyway. But while I might not have the courage for the speech right now, I'm definitely going through with the escape plan I thought up last night when I couldn't sleep.

"Focus on your getaway," I say in my most confident voice.

After drying off, I zip myself into my gray polyester pleated uniform skirt. Then I button up my light blue Oxford shirt, leaving the top three buttons undone. Bowing my head, I say out loud: "Please let this be my last year of uniforms. Aphrodite, goddess of all things beautiful, please have mercy on my wardrobe."

Every year a few of the parents start a petition that high school students should also wear uniforms, but so far, thankfully, it's never passed. Of course, it would be just *my* luck for the school to change its policy next year, when I go to Neapolitan High.

I run my fingers through my hair before slowly approaching my full-length mirror. Breathing in, I slowly take in my reflection. Long brown hair, freckled skin, dolphin-gray eyes, and skinny legs. I sigh because I look exactly like myself. Every summer I hope that the Gods of Puberty and/or Beauty will bestow me with a new look for back to school, but alas, I appear nearly the same as last year. And the year before.

I partly blame the uniform.

How are you supposed to grow up when you're dressing exactly the same as you have since you were *six* years old? Really?

As I apply my lip gloss, I check myself out in the mirror again. Despite recently purchasing a lightly padded bra (a "demi push-up" in Victoria's Secret language), I still totally look like a kid. I guess I *will* be Babylicious forever. At least, after I get to school, I can roll my skirt up a few inches. My mom would murder me if she knew I did that. She specifically bought me new uniform skirts after my recent growth spurt because she deemed last year's skirts "inappropriate, *especially* for someone like you." By "someone like you," she meant the daughter (and star) of MommyliciousMeg.com, a blog with twenty thousand daily readers. Or something roughly around that. I can always tell if my mom's readership is up or down based on what treats she buys from the grocery store. If there are fresh gourmet bakery cookies, it was a good month for readership, therefore advertisers. If it was a bad month, it's Chips Ahoy! all the way.

I clip my bangs to one side with a bobby pin, and I use my magnifying mirror to check for any zits on my face. Every time my mom takes a picture of me, it's always "Get your hair out of your face, sweetie" or "Honey, do you want to borrow some cover-up?" Cover-up is the only makeup that my mom approves of for a fifteen-year-old, and she's always trying to peddle it on me. Sometimes, it seems like I'm not even good enough for my own mom's blog, which is hysterical, since it's *about* me.

I wonder if my mom's hoping that this is the year I finally get pretty. Maybe that would bring in a bigger readership, which seems to be the only thing that makes her happy anymore. Truth Number One of Life with a Blogger: the more website hits, the bigger the smiles. To put it simply, affirmation from random strangers is a total turn-on for my mom.

I take one final look in the mirror before heading down the stairs. Standing at the kitchen counter, I gobble down a bowl of Honey Nut Cheerios with chocolate milk, my all-time favorite breakfast. I can hear my mom upstairs, rustling around in her closet.

I hear a loud *thump*. *Thump*.

This means only one thing: She's getting the tripod out for my "after" back-to-school pictures, the posed ones she takes of me before school when I'm actually standing upright and wearing clothes, not pajamas. She needs the tripod because the point-and-shoot camera isn't good enough on a day like today. Of course, she'll set the timer to get a few posed shots of the two of us together: arms around each other, pretending to be thrilled about going back to school.

Some might think that it's sweet that my mom wants to remember my first day of ninth grade and my last day of uniforms, but it's really not. It's *all* business. Later today, after the photo shoot, she'll upload uncomfortable photos of me and write awkward captions like "Good morning, Babylicious. Love the bed head!" for the "before" photo and "Isn't she filling out nicely?" for the "after" photo. Majorly awkward. Then tonight, my friends and enemies alike will visit her blog and have a nice laugh about it.

But not today.

Today I have an escape route. Even if I'm not ready to confront my mom, I'm still not just going to willingly submit to a back-to-school blog feature.

I open the door that leads to our basement and I tiptoe down the stairs.

Grandma Hope is reclining on her red leather La-Z-Boy. The Golf Channel is on.

She points at an up-and-coming golfer on the screen. "He over-rotates. Why can't anyone but me see that? I've watched this shot *four* times. I'm sure of it. These analysts are all blind bozos. *Where* are the women analysts? They have women on the sidelines at *football* games but not golf matches? That's plain stupid."

She rewinds the screen and presses play. We watch the shot again.

"See. Told you so," she says.

Before she was my grandma, or even my mom's mom, Hope played professional golf in the 1960s; she was part of the early Ladies Professional Golf Association, or the LPGA, as it's better known. When she moved in with us five years ago, right after my grandpa died, she cut back to playing golf four days a week, which doesn't include the days she clocks in at the driving range and the putting green. Luckily, we live in Naples, Florida, where it's summery all year round, so she never has to take a real break from golf. Although she's as healthy as a Florida navel orange in autumn, I think that would kill her.

Diversion, I remember. Concentrate on your escape.

"Grandma Hope, I need your help," I say slowly.

My grandma looks away from the TV and toward me. "Well, don't you look like the bee's knees! That gloss works on you, although I think a Pink Lady–apple red would suit you better. I'm forever confused about your mom's makeup ban. As women, we *still* aren't first-class citizens like men, but at least we get to wear a nice lipstick. Why should your mom deny you that?"

On top of being a terrific athlete, Grandma Hope's also an incredibly classy dame. There isn't a single day where she doesn't dress to impress. Depending on her outfit, she wears either a strand of black pearls or a chunky turquoise necklace. And she always applies her favorite red lipstick, Ruby Slipper, while she's still in bed. I've never *seen* her natural lip color before. Seriously. She keeps a tube of lipstick on her nightstand at all times. And one in her purse, and one in her glove compartment. Her hair is also permanently styled and highly flammable due to her heavy-handed sprays of Aqua Net. "Just because I'm an athlete, doesn't mean I'm a tomboy," she always says.

"Grandma Hope!" I repeat. "I need to be quick. Ninth grade is an *extremely, majorly* big deal, but my mom is driving me crazy by making today about *her* and *her blog*. So will you please, *pretty* please with a cherry on top, drive me before my mom has a chance to make *me* her next photo spread? She already totally ambushed me once today when I was still asleep."

Grandma Hope shuts off the TV, which shocks me. Whenever she's not out on the golf course herself, the Golf Channel is always on. It's the soundtrack of her life; she even raises the volume when she's in the shower. It can get so loud that we can hear it all the way upstairs.

She stares at me from her perch on the couch. "Darling. I have a *crazy* idea: Why don't you just try *talking* to her? Lord knows that I've tried, but I think it needs to come from you. You're her daughter. I'm her mother, so that means she hasn't listened to a single thing I've said since, well, since she was your age."

I pause.

Grandma Hope would love my "Can this year be different?" speech I've been preparing. She'd be so proud of me, especially during the parts in which I stand up for myself and explain why I need my privacy. But I'm not ready for that speech quite yet. Asking someone to stop doing what she has always done is a fairly large request. It's especially tricky to ask your own mother if she'll stop being herself from now on . . . or at least stop being the Mommylicious version of herself.

"I'm not talking to her today, Grandma Hope. There's enough going on already," I answer. "But can you please just help me skip the 'after' pictures? Maybe it'll be an 'Actions speak louder than words' kind of moment."

"All right," Grandma Hope says with a nod. "But you can't hide *forever*."

With the spring of a woman who's had two hole-in-ones in her seventies (and she's only seventy-three), my grandma grabs her keys and the gold chain that dangles with them, and her two most recent hole-in-one balls. She squints at the sun as she peers through the sliding glass doors that lead out to our side yard.

She raises her eyebrows and winks her left eye. "It does look like a swell day for a drive. Do you have your school-bag and your things for swim practice, Georgia?"

My grandma never took to the name Imogene. She is still more than a little bit "salty" (her word, not mine) that my mom chose my name by holding a contest on her blog. So ever since I was little, Grandma Hope's always called me Georgia, my middle name.

I motion to a Vineyard Vines tote bag with a starfish border, a gift from one of my mom's sponsors, and my blue swim bag that constantly reeks of chlorine despite the fact I wash my swimsuits out with a little vinegar to try to get rid of the smell.

"Got the bags. Thanks, Ace," I say. I use my grandma's golf nickname because I know she loves it. Ace, in golf language, is a hole-in-one.

We quietly exit through the sliding doors and make a quick getaway to Grandma's old boat of a convertible, a 1960 Ford Galaxie Sunliner. It's sea-foam green and gorgeous. She already promised me that I can have it when I turn sixteen, but only if I drive her to her golf club, the Orange Grove, whenever she wants.

"You can be my designated driver, and I can finally play the nineteenth hole. I think at seventy-three years old, I've earned that right," she has told me at least a dozen times.

The nineteenth hole is when golfers gather in the clubhouse after playing and socialize over a round of adult beverages. My best friend Sage's grandpa speaks Chinese; my grandma speaks golf. I'm happy to speak Pig Latin in a Romanian accent if it means I get a vintage convertible as my first car. Plus, I'll finally be able to avoid Mommylicious without needing to find a getaway car and a driver.

As my grandma's car is backing down the driveway and only narrowly avoiding our mailbox, my mom, dressed only in her sunflower robe, rushes out our front door like someone just told her George Clooney was shirtless on our front lawn. My mom drives my grandma batty with her clothing choices. "Working from home isn't an excuse to dress homeless," Grandma Hope always lectures her.

I roll down the window, which I do only for effect, since it's a convertible and the top is currently down.

I yell, "I needed to get to school early, so Grandma's taking me!"

"But . . . ," my mom starts to call.

We can't hear the rest of what she says because Grandma Hope has already pressed hard on the accelerator, and we're flying down Mullet Lane, the street I've grown up on since I was born. (Mullets are a local fish.)

I twist around in my seat just long enough to see my mom holding her camera up and taking a picture of us zooming into the distance.

I can almost hear the *click*.

That's not going to be pretty, I think as I turn back around in my seat.

"Your mom will get over it," Grandma Hope says. She takes her right hand off the wheel and gives my knee a tiny squeeze. "Your mom seems to think the blog is a way to keep you hers forever, but you're growing up, and she finally needs to learn to give you some space."

I watch my mom get smaller and smaller in the side mirror. As much as I detest my mom's blog, I also still hate disappointing her. I only wish she had a career other than exploiting me.

Chapter Two

THIS YEAR WILL BE BETTER, RIGHT?

I TEXTED SAGE, MY BEST FRIEND, THAT I'D BE GETTING TO SCHOOL early, so she's already waiting for me in front of St. Augustine Academy when Grandma Hope's car pulls in. By "pulls in," I mean her convertible zooms into the parking lot like it's a speedboat full of cocaine and we're running from the Drug Enforcement Agency. And even though the lot is nearly empty, Grandma chooses one of the few spots clearly labeled FACULTY ONLY.

My grandma definitely doesn't work at my school.

I wish I had inherited her fearlessness, along with her straight, thick hair and long, skinny fingers.

Sage's holding her phone in a tight fist, and she looks pissed. At five feet zero inches tall, Sage is the shortest girl in our class; she always has been and probably always will be. She has a theory on why this is: "If only my mom would let me eat food with fat, I wouldn't be this tiny."

Sage marches right up to the Green Whale (that's my name for grandma's car, although Grandma Hope calls it Green Sherbet Delight). By the time Sage reaches us, she has relaxed her scowl and plants a peck on my grandma's cheek.

Despite being small, Sage is a force to be reckoned with. Her unruly dark brown ringlets take up a lot of surface area, and nobody ever forgets her. Whenever anyone teases me about my mom's blog, Sage always has my back. "Imogene can't choose her mom's job. She wishes her mom wasn't a mommy blogger as much as you wish your dad wasn't a gynecologist," she told Todd Waltman, an annoying kid who thankfully moved to Omaha, Nebraska.

"Morning, darling," Grandma Hope sings out to Sage. "I just can't believe that you girls are in the ninth grade. It seems like *I* was in ninth grade only a day or two ago. I was major trouble that year."

Grandma Hope is always referring to her youth and how wild she was, but she never tells any actual stories. My mom says that it's all an exaggeration, but the way Grandma drives and the way she golfs, I'm not so sure.

Sage flashes her memorable gap-toothed smile and waves good-bye to Grandma Hope, who's already jerked her car into reverse.

"Bye, Basil," my grandma teases Sage. Every time my grandma sees Sage, she calls her by a different herb. Last week, it was thyme. The week before, it was rosemary.

As soon as the Green Whale drives out of sight, Sage re-furrows her dark, thinly plucked eyebrows.

"I have a serious problem," she says, and huddles close to me. Sage points at the touch screen on her phone. It's on her mom's Facebook profile.

Zoey Carter's (Sage's mom's) status reads: "Sent Sage off to her first day of ninth grade with this spinach and kale smoothie. Yum!!! I know . . . I'm the best mom ever! Just say *adios* to sugary cereals and *hola!* to veggies. Join my revolution!"

Linked to the post, there's a photograph of Sage drinking a giant green smoothie out of a milkshake glass with a stalk of celery sticking up like a straw. In the photo, Sage's making a face that looks like she's a contestant on *Fear Factor* and she's being forced to eat cobra eyes.

Except unlike on *Fear Factor,* there's no prize.

Sage's mom is also a blogger.

Her online moniker is VeggieMom because she's a vegan blogger. She photographs and blogs every single item of food that she and Sage eat. Believe it or not, there are lots of bloggers like her; they're usually called food or healthy-living bloggers, and their entries are called food diaries.

Ms. Carter and my mom were actually "blog friends" before they met in real life. That means they met over the internet and became virtual "friends" before ever meeting in person. My mom hasn't met many of her readers, or "friends" as she prefers to call them, but our moms met in real life after Sage and her mom moved from Minneapolis to Florida. Sage's mom was new to the area and lonely, so she emailed my mom, who she knew also lived in Naples. They became fast real-life friends, so Sage and I have grown up both on the internet and in real life together.

Because our moms are both bloggers, sometimes I think that Sage is the only person who at least *sort of* understands me . . . except I'd gladly switch places with her, because at least VeggieMom only blogs about food, and my mom blogs *everything* about me.

After staring at the large glass of greenness on Sage's iPhone, I start to feel a bit nauseous, so I press the home button to exit out of the screenshot.

"I thought she promised no more Facebook updates or Tweets about you. Isn't the blog enough?"

Sage shakes her head and takes her phone back. "*Exactly*. This is only day three, and she's already broken the agreement. But I can't say I'm surprised. It's so *her* to do something like this."

"Totally annoying," I say as we walk toward the

school's entrance. "I escaped with Ace from this morning's photo shoot. I just couldn't do it today. The idea of posing and smiling for my mom's camera makes me want to gag nearly as much as thinking about that green goo you had to swallow."

"You've got to stand up to her," Sage says. "She might not hear you, but at least you can get it out of your system." Sage's always been so much better at telling her mom how she feels. Most of the time, I'd just rather change the subject and avoid talking about how I feel.

"That's pretty much what my grandma said this morning."

I playfully bat Sage's hand. "Sage, stop picking at your fingers." Sage is a competitive piano player who tears at the skin around her nails when she's nervous. "You don't want to be known at Juilliard as the girl with the messed-up fingers."

Sage throws up her scabby hands. "Imogene, you know that just because I'm *good* at the piano, doesn't mean I'll get into Juilliard, right? That only happens in the movies. If I really wanted to get into Juilliard, I'd be playing the piano right now. I'd have to even play when I was supposed to be asleep." She mimics playing the piano with her eyes closed, and I laugh.

Sage sighs. "Maybe at the very best, I'll get into a college with a solid piano major, but I'll *never* get into a conservatory. And besides, how are my mom and I going to afford *any* college?"

Sage's mother is a single mom, and her blog is much less well known and visited than my mom's, so she makes a lot less income from it. Money in their family is always tight. Recently they had to sell their house, which had the most amazing Hass avocado tree in the backyard. They moved into an apartment complex, which was tricky because they had to make sure their new neighbors were okay with hearing classical piano three to four hours a day. Luckily, this is Naples, Florida, and the median age here is sixty-four years old. They found a place where the neighbors in nearly every direction turned out to be both ancient and hard of hearing.

"Well, I totally think you could get into Juilliard or any other college," I tell her honestly. "You're the Nicki Minaj of the piano minus all the costumes, wigs, and expletives . . . but college is a long way off. Let's just focus on having the best year ever before we all go off to high school. Maybe this year I can finally be known as someone more than Babylicious, the girl on that blog."

"Here's hoping," Sage whispers. "And maybe this will be the year I finally get to decide for once what I ingest and what I expel."

★ ★ ★

The first half of the day, I spend worrying about what my mom's going to say when I get home. When our wireless goes down or I spoil a photo op, like I did this morning, she goes into a total tizzy. I guess that saying "Don't take your work home with you" isn't easy to live by when you blog about being a mom. When we eat dinner, it's "How did you like that new Dip & Squeeze Heinz ketchup? I need to review it." We even take sponsored vacations. Our lives move around the blog like it's a permanent fixture. Even though it's usually sunny in Florida, it's always the one cloud in my sky.

I sigh with relief when it's time for my English class, which is the final class of the day and my favorite subject. I love reading books about other periods in history, specifically the Time Before the Internet. I love English class because I get to read about people who just lived *without* documenting every minuscule detail to share with the whole wide world. My mom claims *blog* wasn't even a word until she was twenty-five years old, but I've never known the world without the internet. According to Mommylicious lore, my first word was even *blog*.

Ms. Herring greets all of us as we come into the classroom. "Hello, Imogene," she says.

Our school is tiny, so everyone knows everyone, especially if you're the girl whose mom writes a blog about her.

Ms. Herring's our school's youngest teacher by about a century. All the girls love her because she's fashionable, and all the boys love her because she's beautiful. (Some of our teachers are nuns, so it's hard to get a good gauge of what they actually look like under their habits.) I've been excited to have Ms. Herring since she moved here from Missouri five years ago, so I walk into class with a huge smile on my face—and not just because Dylan Mulberry, my biggest crush of all time, stared at me from across the lunchroom earlier. Or at least, I think he did. He could've been looking at the wall behind me instead.

I take a seat next to Sage in the front row, and I pull out a notebook that someone sent my mom. Companies send her free products in hopes that she'll write about them on her blog—basically, on any given day, I'm a walking billboard. Today I'm wearing shoes donated from Sears (gold penny loafers that are thankfully cute), and this morning I actually washed my hair with those Bubble & Bee products we received last week. (In my opinion, organic is not always better. There were some serious tangles.) I know that I should be happy we get free things, but we don't need or want half of them anyway. Our front closet looks like a fancy 7-Eleven.

"Class," Ms. Herring says in a soft voice. Everyone's chatter stops, and all eyes go to our teacher.

Behind me, I hear the door shut, and I turn to watch

Dylan glide into an empty seat in the back row. He's the cutest guy in the ninth grade—or at least, he's got my vote. With eyes the color of green sea glass, sandy blond hair, and a tan that doesn't even fade in January, he could be on a postcard for Florida. Maybe he and Mickey should team up as our state's ambassadors. Dylan would definitely lure quite a few tourists in with his smile.

I count silently and realize that I have *three* classes with Dylan this year; that's two more than in eighth grade. Hopefully, this will help facilitate my plan to get him to ask me to the Halloween Pirate's Booty Ball. It's our first date dance *ever*.

Ms. Herring pulls down the projector screen. "I just *love* the first day of school. Bobby, please get the lights."

The classroom darkens, and Ms. Herring sits down at her computer desk. "A new school year means new ideas," she says. "I like to switch it up. Otherwise, it gets boring and stale for all of us. Déjà vu isn't a good feeling when it comes to learning." She taps away at her keyboard and then a website that I'm way too familiar with pops up on the projector: It's a website that helps people create blogs.

"This year, instead of writing in journals or typing essays, each student is going to write and maintain his or her own blog. I think it's going to be an *awesome* project."

Whenever a teacher uses *awesome*, students everywhere should be terrified.

She smiles at both Sage and me. Everyone, including Ms. Herring, knows that our moms are bloggers. Not only do our moms give presentations about blogging at career day every year, but they also plug their blogs to anyone who will listen. My mom even has a magnetic MommyliciousMeg.com decal that takes up the entire left side of our car. (I know, mortifying, right? I always sit on the right side of the car to avoid seeing the curious stares from other cars' passengers.)

Why would either Sage or I need any more blogs in our lives?

To my left, Ardsley Taylor raises her hand with the perfect posture of a beauty queen. If our school were cast in a teen movie, Ardsley would play the popular girl who everyone wants to be, even though she's not very nice.

"Ms. Herring, do Sage and Imogene have to write blogs too? Or can they just turn their mothers' blogs in for credit?"

The class begins to snicker, but Ms. Herring puts her finger to her lips and the class quiets. "Ardsley!" Ms. Herring scolds.

"I was just asking a question," Ardsley says in a singsong voice.

I refuse to turn around and acknowledge Ardsley. Ever since she was allowed to use a computer, she's been ragging on me about my mom's blog. My mom said Ardsley would grow out of it, but of course, she hasn't. Despite what parents tell us, people rarely seem to grow out of who they are. And I can't exactly blame Ardsley for teasing me. My mom keeps giving her too much good material. Take my mom's post about my first period, for instance. Two years later, the headline "Babylicious Is Now a Woman" still loops in my nightmares. The day after the post went viral, someone (I suspect Ardsley) decorated my locker with a CONGRATULATIONS sign, the silvery, shiny kind you buy at Party City for someone's new baby or retirement.

Totally humiliating.

I turn toward Sage. She looks nearly as green as her morning smoothie. Does Ms. Herring not comprehend how a blog can ruin a childhood?

As class ticks on, Ms. Herring details exactly how our blogs will work. On one group blog, we will post papers and assignments for class. This way, Ms. Herring explains, "We can learn from one another." Aside from our class blog, we are each responsible for writing our own blog, which we can make private with only Ms. Herring able to see it or make public for everyone on the internet to see. Of course, this prompts a "dangers of the internet" discussion, during which Ms. Herring explains how to be safe online.

Why doesn't anyone ever tell *grown-ups* to be safe online? It seems like every night on the news, there's a story about kids being dumb on the internet, but there are never any stories about the ridiculous things parents do online. Namely, join Facebook, friend their own children, and write blogs.

At the end of her spiel, Ms. Herring reminds us that our private blog is extremely important, and drops the bomb that it's worth 25 percent of our entire grade.

Superlicious. That's Sage's and my sarcastic way of saying something is terrible.

After class is dismissed, Sage leans over and whispers, "We need to do something about this, stat. I don't *want* a blog. It's bad enough that my mom has one."

I nod furiously. There's *no* way I'm starting a blog either. This assignment has the potential to make the ninth grade officially the worst, and it's only day one.

So much for the best year ever.

Mommylicious

"MY BABY IS GOING TO HAVE A BLOG!"

You read it here first!!! Mommylicious's Babylicious, Imogene, is starting her own blog! It's for her English class, and I'm thrilled that this is something we can share. Lately she hasn't seemed as interested in my blog (as you might've noticed in the re-created "after" back-to-school shots), so hopefully this will bring us closer again.

According to the email from her English teacher, the blog will have two functions: 1) It will be where she posts papers on books that the class is reading. 2) It will act as a journal of her year.

Basically, I get to read my daughter's diary, and y'all can too! Brilliant! Not to mention that I'm delighted that the school is teaching kids internet skills. Remember the days of blackboards and chalk? Talk about torture in the Old Ages. I <3 the internet.

I think it's so progressive of the school to have students start blogs. As we all know, blogs and blogging communities are majorly powerful. Who would I be without Mommylicious?

Imogene hasn't given me her blog's URL yet, but I know she will soon!

Anyone else's kids have blogs? Here's a philosophical question to chew on: If your baby has a blog, does that mean she's not a baby anymore? Since Imogene deactivated her Facebook account last year, I haven't had a way to connect to her online! *I know.* A blogger whose own kid isn't even on Facebook . . . Talk about irony. So, obviously, this blog project is reason to celebrate, and I'm so excited that I can now proudly call my daughter a fellow blogger.

Unfortunately, in other ironic news, my mom is still refusing to get an email account. "The Golf Channel is all I need," she says. "And a good newspaper." Yup, it's official. . . . I have a dinosaur living in my basement!

Read my review of Bounty's newest line of super-duper absorbent paper towels HERE. They really are the quicker picker-upper.

Butterfly Kisses,
Mommylicious

Chapter Three

ARE YOU MORALLY OPPOSED TO ALGEBRA?

"IMOGENE AND SAGE," FATHER SULLIVAN SAYS STERNLY. "Ms. Herring tells me that neither of you has posted the first two assignments to your blogs. I hope you girls realize that you're required to do your homework, regardless of any personal reservations you might have. And let me remind you both that your grades are now going on your transcript for college applications."

Father Sullivan leans back in his black leather office chair so far that I'm afraid he'll tip over, and I won't be able to laugh because you're not allowed to laugh at your principal, especially not when he's a priest and there are Jesus and Mary statues staring directly at you.

Sage and I don't say a word. We've agreed that we're

only going to start blogging if Father Sullivan threatens suspension. So far, neither he nor Ms. Herring has even sent a note home. We're going to just continue to hand in assignments typed on paper, the good old-fashioned way. Technically, we're still doing the assignments; we're just not posting them to the group blog.

Luckily, the journal part of the blog doesn't start for another week or so. That'll be a whole other battle.

Our thought is that passive resistance will eventually teach Ms. Herring (and our moms) that we don't believe in blogging, and we won't participate in it.

Father Sullivan takes a long sip of water and then wipes a smudge off his glass.

"Girls, I personally disliked algebra, but that doesn't mean I didn't have to take it."

Sage gives me her "I'll handle this one" look, and I don't stop her.

She turns to Father Sullivan and closes her eyes as if she were about to make a confession. She breathes through her nostrils, opens her eyes, and points her finger at Father Sullivan.

"It's not simply that Imogene and I do not *like* blogs; we're *morally opposed* to blogging. Are you *morally opposed* to mathematics?"

"No," Father Sullivan responds, shaking his head. "The Catholic church is not morally opposed to mathematics;

we have much bigger enemies to worry about." He pauses. "Admittedly, I'm not as into technology as the younger teachers, and I don't really get this . . . *blogging*." He pronounces *blogging* as if it were a word from a foreign language.

Sage puts her finger down. And again, I have to cover my mouth and suppress my urge to laugh.

He leans forward in his chair. "But if Ms. Herring wants you two to blog, you will. If I get any more notices that either of you is not blogging, I will call your mothers in for our next meeting. Let's *try* not to have another meeting, girls."

He pauses and scratches his head. "Aren't you part of the YouTube generation? So what's the big deal about posting on the internet? Don't you kids love doing that?"

Not when our moms do it for us, I think.

Sage pushes out her chair. "Thank you for listening to our concerns, Father Sullivan." She says it so sweetly that only her best friend would know that she's being sarcastic.

Father Sullivan smiles, gets up, and firmly shuts his office door behind us as if he's done with both this matter—and us.

Once we're a few steps away, I whisper, "What's our next move?"

Sage pretends to wave a flag. "Surrender?"

"Are you sure, Sage?"

She picks at her fingers. "Do you have any better ideas? I have to get perfect grades if I want to get into a good school with a piano major. And like Father Sullivan said, our grades are actually going on our transcripts for college now that we're in the ninth grade. The stakes are higher. We're not little kids anymore, Imogene."

I gently grab her hand so she can't pick anymore, and we walk toward my locker.

"Okay, we won't do anything to jeopardize Juilliard. I promise."

"Imogene! I'm not getting into Juilliard!" Sage whines, and I laugh because we have this pretend argument all the time.

Since Sage is usually the one with the plan, the one who's always telling *me* to stick up to my mom, I'm starting to get worried. If she's ready to call our passive resistance off, then there's no hope unless *I* can think of something.

I take my swimming bag out of my locker. One of the best parts about Florida is that the schools have outdoor pools. You can get sun *and* fulfill your sports requirement at the same time.

"Let me think about it underwater," I say. Ever since I joined Little Dolphin Swim School when I was four years old, I've always done my best brainstorming while swimming laps. I'm hoping to swim well enough this year to make the varsity team my first year of high school.

"All right," Sage says. "Hatch us up a brilliant idea, my little mermaid, and we'll meet this weekend to discuss. I'm off to play the piano and get one note closer to leaving this place. Somehow I think mastering Liszt might be easier than dealing with my mom. At least our moms won't be able to blog about us when we're off at college."

I hoist my bag over my shoulder. "Don't be so sure that they won't," I warn. "Besides, four years is too long to wait. I'll think of something."

I only wish I felt as confident as I sounded.

After swim practice, I spot my dad's vintage Jeep Wagoneer waiting in our school's parking lot. He toots the horn two times and flags me down. It's slightly embarrassing, but since I usually take the late bus, I'm happy to see him. Typically, my dad works late at his architecture firm, Luden & Cross, so it's unusual for him to surprise me like this.

After I get into the car, I give my dad a smile. "What's up, Dad?"

He starts up the car but doesn't put it in drive. "I had a rough day at the office, and I thought picking *you* up might pick *me* up."

Yup, my dad's *totally* corny, like out-of-a-family-sitcom corny.

But unlike most parents, he's a truth teller. He doesn't

hide anything from me. Sometimes it's great to have a parent treat you like an adult, but other times, it's annoying, because then you have to act like one.

"I'm sorry, Dad."

He hesitates then finally puts the car in drive.

As we pull out of the parking lot and head toward home, I try to gauge his mood. He gets this one wrinkle above his lip when he's super-upset. I start to get *really* worried when I realize it's there . . . big-time.

I run my fingers through my wet hair. "Are you okay, Dad?"

As we drive through historic Naples, the part of town with adorable pastel-colored cottages, expensive shops, and touristy restaurants like Tommy Bahama, I wait for him to answer.

His speckled gray hair is being blown around like crazy since the window's down. He rolls it up and looks over at me. "I have bad news. We lost that big deal," he says. "That big deal" is a project that my dad has been working and bidding on for more than a year—a huge assisted-living development. My dad's firm was in the running to design and build it. I know this development would have been a life raft for my dad's company, which has struggled since the last economic downturn.

I try to put aside my own worries so I can be there for him. I pat my dad on the shoulder. "I'm sorry, Dad," I say.

I wish I knew what would make him feel better. There are all these books and magazines (and, gulp . . . *blogs*) for parents about how to deal with their kids, but how come there aren't any for kids on how to deal with their parents, especially when the parents are the ones who are sad?

My dad grasps my forearm lightly. "We'll be fine, honey. It's fortunate that your mom's blog has been doing so well. It's nice to have a safety net to fall back on. Not every family is so fortunate." He glances over at me with a forced smile. "And, hey, what's this I hear about your English class starting blogs?"

Because I hate my mom's blog so much, I forget that it's become a business, and that we depend on it for money sometimes. After my dad's news, I feel torn about the new idea that came to me during our long set in swim practice. But I don't feel torn enough that I won't run it past Sage.

Mommylicious

"It's Not Always Sunny in Florida"

The Hubby, as he's known affectionately around here, has been having a rough go at work lately. Since I'm a *mommy* blogger, I try not to focus on him too much in the blog unless it's about him being *Daddylicious*. But please, everyone put some good thoughts into the blogosphere for him. We all know the power of positivity. I thank you in advance!

If you want to read our HOW WE MET story, click HERE. I promise it's a good one. Think fate, serendipity, and destiny rolled into one. (Anyone know any Hollywood producers who are looking for a romantic-comedy plotline?)

Before I forget, the big news is that it's Tip Thursday (!!!), which for all you new readers (WELCOME!!!) is the day I offer a parenting tip. After all, the whole reason I write this blog is to share what I've learned in this crazy journey called Mommyhood.

Tip #232: Mommy Does Always Know Best.

As regular readers know, Imogene's growing up. Thanks to fellow mommy bloggers at Mommies"R"Us, I know that I'm not the *only one* with a hormonal teenager. Every year, Imogene comes to BlogHer with me. This year BlogHer is being held in Minneapolis, the hometown of my bestie, VeggieMom! (Thanks, Pampers, for sponsoring our trip! Play. Laugh. Grow.)

Anyway, at our house it's all coming to a breaking point, because this year Imogene keeps saying she doesn't want to attend BlogHer. At first I tried listening to her excuses and seeing if she had an actual reason for not wanting to go. I'm a big believer in "Listen first, act second" parenting. But Imogene's excuses just did not seem valid. First, she had a lot of homework, then a very important social event, and finally she said: "I just don't feel like it."

Number One Worst Kid Excuse Ever: "I just don't feel like it."

This is the moment when I realized Tip #232: Mommy Does Always Know Best. Imogene will be coming to BlogHer with me. We don't stop a wonderful mother-daughter tradition and an opportunity to network with our fans and community just because she "doesn't feel like it." Plus, I would be lost without Imogene at BlogHer. It's my favorite bonding weekend of the year. In four years, when she's off at college (insert big tear!), she can make her own decisions. But right now, Imogene is under my roof, so it's still mommy dearest's call.

I know when Imogene becomes a mother herself in the years to come (let's hope the decades to come), she'll finally understand that mommies do know best. . . . Until then, she'll just have to deal with it.

To all the mommies out there, stay strong. Who's the boss? *You're* the boss!

Butterfly Kisses,
Mommylicious

Chapter Four

THE MOMMY BLOGGERS' DAUGHTERS

AT THE COASTLAND CENTER, OUR LOCAL MALL, I FIND SAGE sitting at a table on the perimeter of the food court, drinking an Orange Julius and eating a Mrs. Fields peanut butter cookie.

"Sorry," she says between bites and sips. "I was starving. I couldn't wait any longer—not even a nanosecond."

I steal a slug of her extra-large Orange Julius. "No worries, Sage. I've had dinner at your house. I completely agree that tofu should be banned, especially after tasting that Tofurky your mom brought to Thanksgiving last year. The pilgrims *and* the Native Americans would have been majorly appalled."

"Is this it? Are we done for?" Sage asks. "Are we

going to end our passive resistance and just start blogging?" She says *blogging* like it's a word that shouldn't be uttered in polite company—you know, the type that gets bleeped on TV.

For Sage and me, sometimes *blog* does feel like a curse word. "It's for my blog" has to be my least favorite sentence ever.

I catch Sage staring at me with the same look she had when she lost the election for student council president last year. (She lost to Ardsley, who ran on a "TV and Starbucks Frappuccino study break" platform, even though everyone knew that the administration would never allow it.)

I smile. "Sage, you might not believe this, but I actually have an *incredible* idea."

Sage raises her eyebrows since her mouth is now full, and she makes a motion with her hand for me to get on with it.

My heart starts to race. Somehow I just feel like this idea could change my year—and Sage's year too.

Sage covers her mouth with her hand because she's still chewing. "Spit it out, Imogene."

"Okay, okay. If we're forced to write blog entries about our life, then let's *really* write about our lives. Everyone else is planning on keeping theirs private. We know all too well that the point of a blog is to be public—and ours would *have* to be public. And this is the *genius* part. Instead of writing generic material like 'I went to school, and it was chicken nugget day. Score,' let's promise to write the truth, the whole truth, and nothing but the truth, about our home lives, *specifically* about our moms. They'll stop blogging about us in no time once they realize how sucky it feels."

I hand a piece of paper outlining my plan to Sage. The heading reads "How We Fight Back." I detail how we'll both blog about our lives and call ourselves the Mommy Bloggers' Daughters.

Sage reads the paper, shakes her head, and giggles. "No way, Imogene," she says. "We're teenagers. No one wants us to be honest with anyone. Plus, you're *scared* of your mom. How would you ever pull this off? You can't even talk to her."

"*News flash*: Nobody should share their life with the World Wide Web," I say, performing a 360-degree eye roll. "That's the whole point of all this. We're just going to give our moms a taste of their own medicine, or in your mom's case, health food. All these years, they've written about us twenty-four-seven. Now it's our turn to write about *them*. I'm pretty sure that it will be easier to write about them online than it would be to actually talk to them in person. And *the* bestest part is that we get school credit for it. These blogs are going to guarantee us As in English class *and* solve our mom issues."

My idea sounds even better out loud than it did when I thought of it during the dolphin dive lap. Maybe I used to be a fish in a past life, and that's why I can think so well underwater.

I hear a sucking noise as Sage drains the last of her Orange Julius, then hands the paper back to me.

She tosses her curls over her shoulder. "I'm not so sure," she says.

I never even thought about the possibility that Sage wouldn't go for it—*she's* the brave one. "It's for school. They can't get that mad," I add, even though I'm not so sure about that.

Sage is totally right that I'm a little scared of my mom, but I'm also afraid that nothing will ever change if I don't *do* something.

After all, my dad always says to fight fire with fire. Why didn't I think of this idea before?

Ever since I can remember, Sage and I have mostly tried to avoid, rather than attract, extra attention *because* of our moms' blogs. This would be going against all that. But maybe it's time. Maybe it's not *this year* that's going to be different—maybe it's *me* who's going to be different.

Sage looks at me as if I'm tempting an alligator with a fish. Her eyes are wide open, and if eyes could actually talk, hers would be screaming, *This is an epically bad idea— like, even more bad than the time I ate two corn dogs three minutes before going on Rip Ride Rockit at Universal Studios.*

Sage and her talking eyes are probably right. This strategy could be really stupid. I should probably just accept that my mom's always going to blog about me. She'll probably even blog about *my* kids one day. Is there such a thing as a grandmommy blogger?

Plus, I probably shouldn't rock the boat, considering my dad's situation.

And if Sage isn't in, there's no way I'm going to do it on my own.

I roll up the papers. "Fine. Let's surrender. Do you happen to have a white flag in your purse?"

Sage stands up. "Don't give in that easily," she says. "Your mom's not *that* terrifying." She points toward the other end of the food court. "Wait with me in line for Sbarro? I'm still starving."

Sage is as skinny as a prepubescent celebrity, which makes sense because she hates healthy food, and that's all that her mom serves. But sometimes I think Sage goes on total junk-food sprees more because she's angry with her mom than because she's actually hungry.

I push my orange plastic chair out and chase after Sage, who's quickly making her way across the food court.

We get in line behind a young, blond Lululemon-exercise-clothes-wearing mom. She's pushing two infants in a double stroller and an adorable toddler in seersucker overalls is trailing behind.

"I'm not scared of Mommylicious," I argue, turning to Sage. "It's just that things are complicated at home."

"Do you think I don't know about what's going on at home?" Sage asks.

I stare at the pizza under the heat lamps instead of making eye contact with Sage.

"*I* didn't tell you about it," I say.

"I read all about the Hubby and his hard time at work this morning on your mom's blog," she says. "I figured your dad lost the assisted-living deal. I know that he was so excited. I mean, he showed us the blueprints five times in one week. I think I almost had them memorized."

"It does stink." I wish that there were something I could do for him. And, on top of everything, I'm sure he hates that my mom is blogging about it. At least, I would.

"My idea is stupid, Sage," I say, remembering my conversation with my dad. "Let's forget about it."

Sage grabs a red tray, moves down the line, and points to a manatee-size slice.

"Pepperoni pizza," she says to the Sbarro's employee. "Stuffed pepperoni pizza, and can I please have that large one over there?"

As Sage's paying the cashier, the woman pushing the twin infants stops and gives me the "I know you" stare. It's a look I know too well.

"Oh em gee!" she squeals. "We just moved here from Columbus, and I thought that there'd be *a chance* we'd run into you or your mom, but I wasn't sure when. Now, on my very first trip to the mall, here you are in the flesh! Wow! And you look so much skinnier in real life, honey. And older, too."

She pulls her toddler closer to her and leans over her fancy double stroller. "Bonds, Gardner, and Jack, this is Babylicious. I learned everything about being a good mommy from her mommy, Mommylicious," she coos in a baby voice.

The woman doesn't ask me anything about myself. She doesn't even introduce herself or her three kids. It's as if people think that just because they read about me on the internet, they know me, and that through some internet magic, I know them. They also all seem to believe that Mommylicious is some parenting genius/guru/goddess.

That's the most insane part of it all.

I feel like the man behind the curtain in Oz. Should I reveal to her that it's all fake? Should I tell her Mommylicious and Babylicious only go on "mommy and baby dates" because my mom bribes me? Should I mention that I grind my teeth every time I smile for one of my mom's photos? Seriously. I'm going to need dentures before I even graduate from college.

I nearly open my mouth, but Sage balances her tray

with one hand and starts to pull me away with her other. But just as I start to follow, she hesitates. This would not be the first time Sage confronted someone who thought they knew either her or me because of our mom's blogs. She was grounded for two weeks when someone emailed VeggieMom about an uncomfortable encounter with Sage at Quiznos. (And, to make it worse, they ratted her out for eating a cookie that wasn't made only from quinoa and kale!)

"Sage, don't," I whisper.

But she's already letting go of me and setting her tray back down.

Sage points her finger at me without taking her eyes off the woman. "Just so you know, Imogene the person and Imogene from Mommylicious are actually two entirely separate people." She makes the number two with her fingers in case the woman was confused.

Luckily, Sage stops there. The baffled young mother stands frozen in place. I *almost* feel bad and briefly remember when I actually *liked* people stopping me about the blog. As a little girl, I thought I was lucky because I was the star of Mommylicious. I'd pose for pictures with my hand on my hip and a big smile across my face. I thought that my mom wrote a blog about me because she loved me so much and because I was special. What was I thinking? And why was I smiling?

I pull Sage away from the wreckage she's created.

She sighs. "Let's do it."

"I'm in," I say.

"Class," Ms. Herring says.

All the girls look up at her while the boys' eyes remain firmly on the bit of cleavage that her cardigan reveals.

"Class!" she repeats. I watch as some of the boys' eyes rise a tiny bit. Ugh—boys.

"I know it's Friday, but please at least *pretend* to concentrate," Ms. Herring begs. "For this weekend's homework, you will be writing your first post on your blog. From now until the end of the year, you will be required to write at least one entry per week. Please, please remember that you shouldn't write anything on a blog that you wouldn't tell someone to their face with fifty people watching."

Duh. Someone should tell that to the mommy bloggers of the world. Again, my point is made. It's adults, not teenagers, who need the lessons in social media.

"If you don't know what's appropriate for the public, keep your settings on private," Ms. Herring repeats for about the five hundredth time since she announced the assignment. Then she reiterates six examples of celebrities who misused social media and got into trouble.

It's been a week since I wrote "The Mommy Bloggers' Daughters" rules for me and Sage.

49

Rule Number One is that if something happens at home, you must write about it with total honesty.

Rule Number Two is that when it comes to school matters, particularly matters of the heart, it's okay to be vague.

"After all," I wrote, "we're trying to prove a point, not commit social suicide before high school even begins." I specifically wrote this part so I didn't have to go all "Dear Diary" about my crush on Dylan and how much I want him to ask me to the Pirate's Booty Ball. I also think that Sage is developing a major crush on another boy in our class, Andrew, so I'm saving her, too.

Sage walks over to my locker after class. She twirls one of her ringlets. "Of course, my mom's totally stoked for me to have a blog. She even wants me to print up business cards and hand them out at BlogHer. My mom has no idea that she's definitely not going to want *anyone* to read my blog. *She's* not even going to want to read it. By the way, you are *not* skipping the conference. I mean, who will I make fun of all the blogsters with if you're not there?"

I grab my swim bag from the bottom of my locker and shut the door with a *bang*.

"Of course I'll be going. I have no choice. Didn't you read parenting rule number two hundred and thirty-two? Mommy *does* always know best. Her words, *not* mine. Obvi."

Despite trying to get out of BlogHer, I know that I'll be

attending because Mommylicious always wins. BlogHer is like the prom of all blogging events. But I find it totally boring, and I spend most my time dodging crazy readers. Some of them actually ask for our autographs. Mega-weird. Anyone can have a blog, so it's definitely not special to have one. And why in the world does anyone care about my mom's life? Or mine? From personal experience, I can tell you that it's between moderately and extremely boring.

Sage waves her hand in front of my face. "Hi!" she says, trying to get my attention again. "Imogene, please listen to me! I *just* said, 'Guess who's having a pool party at his house the weekend after this one?'"

"*No way,*" I say, and throw my bag over my shoulder. "There's no way Dylan is having a party. He's never had a party."

Dylan's always been a bit of a mystery. Back when everyone invited the whole class to birthday parties, Dylan never even had one to invite *anyone* to. His parents are both big-shot businesspeople and travel a lot, so maybe that's why.

"Andrew told me that's what he heard," Sage says. Andrew plays the violin, so sometimes he and Sage hang out where they take lessons. Sage still won't publicly—or even privately—admit to having crushed on him for years. She's surprisingly shy like that.

"Andrew says Dylan's inviting, like, everyone, so I guess that includes us, too."

Between worrying about this whole blog assignment and how hard my dad's job is right now, this is the best news of the school year so far.

"Hey, is it weird that I care most about what kind of food is going to be there?" Sage asks.

"It's not," I say, "especially considering what you ate for dinner. Seaweed salad? It looked like food for Flipper the dolphin."

I'm happy that my mom relaxed the healthy-eating blog angle after I was born. I'm not a big fan of vegetables, especially when they grow on the ocean's floor.

When we reach the pool's entrance, Sage waves goodbye. "I'll see you next week. This is our weekend to work at the community farm. Isn't life sweet as a vegan?" She smiles. "I mean, naturally sweet, of course, since sugar is a total no-no. I'm heading out, but I'm very excited to read your first post, Babylicious!"

"Bye-bye, VeggieBaby," I call.

Although I hate it when people call me Babylicious to my face, I don't mind it when it's Sage, who does it because she's the only person I know who actually understands that I'm *not* Babylicious. To Sage, I'm Imogene, her best friend—not just the girl on that blog.

Chapter Five

"REVENGE," SHE TYPES

"IMOGENE!" MY MOM HOLLERS DOWNSTAIRS INTO THE BASEMENT, where I'm hiding out with Grandma Hope.

"What?" I yell back.

Grandma Hope turns up the volume on the Golf Channel so loud that a golf ball being hit sounds nearly the same as a cannon firing.

I take the hint and head up the stairs.

"Honey, in here!" my mom calls from her blogging enclave, a former guestroom that my dad converted into her office.

Tacked against the wall is a giant printed sign of the Mommylicious logo and URL from last year's BlogHer booth. My mom's also blown up and framed a professional headshot. It's literally larger than life. Her eyes are the same size as clementines, and they're staring directly at me.

Yes, it's very scary.

There are also coffee cups, baby bottles, sippy cups, stickers, and buttons emblazoned with the Mommylicious logo littered everywhere. The room looks like a campaign office in November right before an election. "The first step of publicity is attaching your image to your message," as my mom always says.

I focus on a red beanbag chair that sits to the left of my mom's desk. I used to call it "my office chair" back when I hung out in here while my mom worked. That was back when I was still all about being Babylicious, before I realized she was a character that my mom invented. She's the pretty, perfect version of me whose problems always seem to be miraculously solved by Mommylicious's next post.

I stand there, waiting, and also wondering why she's never gotten rid of the beanbag chair, especially since I haven't sat on it for years. The shape of my ten-year-old butt is probably still imprinted in it.

My mom's head is about an inch from the computer screen; she hasn't even looked my way once since I walked into the room.

"*Mom,*" I say loudly.

She continues to tap away quickly at the computer keys until she finally swivels her chair around and faces me.

"Imogene, I haven't seen much of you since school started, and I know that I was pretty upset about the whole 'after' picture thing." She rolls her chair toward me. "Maybe I was a little too upset," she says.

Wait—is it possible that my mom is about to apologize? Has my idea somehow begun to work before it even started?

"So . . . ," my mom continues, "I have a fabulous idea. How would you like to spend a weekend with me at a four-star resort and spa in Key West soon? They've been begging me to review them for years." My mom clasps her hands in excitement. "Doesn't that sound awesome? We could catch up and I could hear how your *last* year before high school is going. . . . I still can't believe how fast time is flying. And you could try out some of those swimsuits that new company sent you. The readers just *love* your reviews, honey."

Of course this is why she wanted to talk to me.

I should've known better than to think my mom was actually apologizing. She just wants Babylicious content, and I already told her five times I don't want to review swimsuits or anything else.

"Mom," I say, stepping back from her grasp. "I'm sorry, but I can't go to Key West. I have schoolwork. Swim team. Friends. I can't just go away for a weekend right now."

I want to start in with my speech about privacy and about how it feels as if she doesn't actually want to spend time with me, that she just wants to get Babylicious posts, but I leave it at that. I'll let my blog do the talking. That sounds easier.

"I'm sure Sage wouldn't miss you for one weekend. She'd understand," my mom says, and turns back around to face her computer. Within a second, she's typing again.

"Yes, Sage does understand," I say. "She understands exactly what it's like to have no control over your own life," I add under my breath, way too softly for my mom to hear.

I back out of her office door. "I have to go do some homework, Mom."

After retreating to my room, I text Sage:

It's on.

I open my laptop and start writing.

The Mommy Bloggers' Daughters: The Girl on That Blog

"Multigenerational Living"

My grandma Hope, also known as Ace, moved in with my family four years ago when my grandpa Fred passed away. She lives in our basement, but it's probably not the dark-dungeon type of basement you're thinking of. My dad's an architect and he designed our house, so it's a *really* nice walk-out basement.

Mom had me convinced that she knew best before. But once my grandma came to stay, I realized that it was really *Grandma Hope* who knew what was up.

Even though my mom pretends that she didn't exist before she met my dad and started her blog, she actually did exist. My grandma has all the awkward photos in boxes to prove it. I'll post some later, so stay tuned! Let's just say the eighties hair is even crazier than it looks in the movies.

This one is the best: Even though my mom pretends to be a genius about all things mommy, I found out that she actually used to call my grandma every day crying and asking her questions about being a parent. So she isn't nearly as confident as she makes herself seem on her blog.

That's all for now. Any readers out there learn anything from living in a multigenerational family?

Skulls and Bones,

Don't Dare Call Me Babylicious

The Mommy Bloggers' Daughters:
Life with VeggieMom

"What VeggieMom Forgot to Mention"

My mom runs VeggieMom, which is a blog about being a vegan single mom in Florida. Even though my mom argues for total transparency and honesty on her blog, here are a few things she forgot to mention last year.

She cried on Valentine's Day and ate Ben & Jerry's from the carton, which is something I would be undoubtedly grounded for. Great double standards.

Her fancy lipstick, which she wears on dates with "winners," is not organic. She buys it at drugstores, and I imagine child workers in China manufacture it. So much for her revolution.

That's all for now. Off to work at the farm!

VeggieBaby Fights Back!

Chapter Six

THE FALLOUT

WHEN I GET TO SCHOOL ON MONDAY, SAGE IS SITTING OUTSIDE on a bench near a fountain adorned with naked cherubs.

She stands up and starts a slow clap as I approach. "Wow! You have more guts than I thought. Like *tons* more. I'm super-impressed."

I can't help smiling. Sage has always been the brave, outspoken one, so it's nice to get courage kudos from her.

"I learned how to be brave and bold from you," I say. "But I still never thought you'd bring up Valentine's Day."

"I only added that part after my mom went totally psycho on me because she found a Skittles wrapper in my room. It was only a fun-size one too. She'd rather me swim with sharks or do meth than eat processed sugar. She might even believe that if we all didn't eat sugar, there'd be world peace. She's delusional."

Sage pulls out a Tootsie Roll from a side zipper on her backpack. "Clearly, chocolate is the key to peace," Sage says with a laugh as she unwraps her candy. "Anyway, we'll find out this afternoon what we're in for at home. I'm sure my mom's going through my computer history right now."

"Totally," I say. "My mom has that software so she knows everything I do on the internet. Like, the program literally records my keystrokes. It's only a matter of time before she sees my blog and freaks, which I guess is the whole point of all this."

As much as I do want my mom to understand how I feel, I'm also scared of what will happen when she does find out.

"How do you think Ms. Herring will react?" Sage asks as we make our way into school.

"I think she's going to want to put the devil back in the box," I say. "We're not the only ones who can learn lessons about social media, right? Hopefully, Ms. Herring will cancel this whole stupid project, our moms will wake up, and we can have a great school year and make people realize before high school that there's more to us than the fact that we're the subjects of our moms' blogs."

The rest of the day continued like most days. Class, PE, and lunch, during which Sage bartered for other people's desserts, and then it was time for English.

Part of me is scared that I have gone too far with my first post, but part of me just thinks I'm doing *exactly* what my mom's always done to me.

There's something strangely liberating about honesty.

When I walk into class, I feel a tap on my shoulder. Turning around, I come face to face with Dylan—*the* Dylan.

"Hi!" I say. Oh em gee, why did I say "hi" like that? I said it as if Dylan was the first person I've seen in years after being deserted on an island. Talk about desperate.

I pause and try to stop panting like I just sprinted the fifty-meter freestyle without taking a single breath.

I'm so hoping that I'm about to get the pool-party invite. In the hallway before class, I'm pretty sure that I overheard Ardsley use the words *Dylan* and *party* together in a sentence. I'll be crushed if she's invited and I'm not.

Dylan smiles at me. He's one of the few kids who never had braces yet still has a perfect smile. Seriously, it's such a good smile. "It's kinda cool that you and your grandma hang out together," he says.

Dylan and I have talked about only six times since the second grade, when we shared a table for two glorious months. That averages out to speaking roughly once a year. So when I said I like him, I should've said that I like him from afar in the hopes of possibly having the chance of liking him up close. I'm really hoping this won't be our one-and-only talk for this year. I'm so ready to beat last year's stats.

"How did you know that my grandma and I hang out?" I say, even though that's the dumbest question ever coming from the daughter of a blogger. Just last weekend, my mom posted no fewer than twenty photos of me cheering on Grandma at her 70+ golf tournament at the Orange Grove. (She won, of course.)

"I saw pictures on your mom's blog. It was up on our family computer. I think my mom reads it sometimes," he says. "Your grandma's swing is murderous. Did she really play in the LPGA?"

For a *very* brief moment, I'm grateful for my mom's blog, because it's the only reason that Dylan is actually talking to me right now.

"She did play professionally," I say. "She's got some pretty great stories about Arnold Palmer."

I'm about to start in on my favorite when Ms. Herring calls out, "Hey, everyone, time to quiet down and get to work."

Turning back toward my seat, I deflate a little that my conversation with Dylan has been cut short, and I haven't been invited to the party.

"Class!" Ms. Herring says.

Nobody's in their seats when the bell rings. Three weeks into the year, and students have already caught the attention-deficit bug. I blame it partly on living in Florida. This state isn't conducive to school or learning. While it's great to live somewhere where it's always warm, it's hard to pay attention somewhere that the sun is always shining and where the beach is ten minutes away.

I smile at Dylan one last time, and I hope that I don't look like a blush experiment gone very badly. Slowly, we all float to our seats, which weren't assigned, but everyone still sits in the same spot every day.

"Let's talk about your experiences with your first personal blog posts," Ms. Herring says.

I look down because I'm afraid she's going to start in on me and Sage. I wish we hadn't sat in the front row on the first day. It was much easier to be brave alone with my computer.

"Dylan," Ms. Herring says, and points toward the back of the classroom.

I whip around to see Dylan raising his hand. The room goes quiet. I think even Ms. Herring is shocked because Dylan never talks in class.

"This is more of a question," Dylan says. "If the blog is supposed to be like a diary, then we should just be writing to ourselves, right? But if it's public, who are we writing to? And why are we sharing our lives with strangers?"

Dylan's hotness just went up tenfold. Why *are* we sharing information with strangers? Why is my life on the internet for any weirdo to look at?

Blogging is confusing.

"That's a great question," Ms. Herring says. "But I don't have any easy answer. It is an important objective in our school that ninth graders become comfortable with writing about their lives before high school, but who you are writing *to* is a personal decision. However, knowing your audience is an extremely important part of writing. Let's look at a few of your classmates' blogs as examples."

She turns off the lights and pulls down the projector screen.

With a few strokes on the computer, our entire class is staring at Sage's blog—and then my blog.

"I wanted to commend both Sage and Imogene for setting their blogs to public. It's very brave."

At first, everyone takes a moment to look at us as if we're sea monsters. Then their eyes shoot back to the projector screen, where there are two windows open. One is open to Sage's blog and the other is open to mine. As the class reads, I watch mouths drop. The Mommy Bloggers' Daughters are officially viral. There's no going back now.

After a few minutes, Ms. Herring turns the lights back on. "So, Imogene . . . Why did you choose to write about your mother? Is she your audience as well as your subject?"

"I'm not . . . s-sure," I stammer. "She's been writing about me for so long that it was nice to finally have my own voice. I just had a lot to say." As I'm speaking, I'm realizing how refreshing it is to finally get to narrate my own life.

That's what's so exciting about this—I finally get to have my say.

This is where I thought Ms. Herring would give us her spiel about how we need to be careful on the internet, how words can damage reputations, how everything we say online is permanent—basically give us our hundredth social media lecture. But she doesn't.

"I want to encourage everyone to be as courageous as Imogene and Sage. Of course, it's up to you all if you want to make your blogs private or public. I don't care either way. But I do want you guys to write about what's personal, and the things that matter to *you*. I hope you take that to heart for the next entry. As much as I enjoy the show, I don't think I need any more posts on *So You Think You Can Dance?* But, yes, I do agree that Leo should've been saved after that amazing modern dance solo."

As the class morphs into a reality TV show conversation, I sit back and realize that for the first time in my school career, I really feel proud of something. I've never been the student whose artwork got displayed in the school lobby or whose essays were handed out as examples of good writing, and I thought that didn't matter to me. But it does—it feels great to be acknowledged. Sage's glowing the same way she did after her last piano recital when she killed her Chopin piece, so I think she feels it too.

After class, as I'm squeezing by Dylan's desk, he reaches up and touches my arm.

"Imogene," he says. "I can't believe how honest you were on your blog. I could never do that. My first entry was just about going paddleboarding, and my blog's not even set to public."

I try not to move an inch and I hope that he'll never let go of my arm.

"Well, that sounds awesome to me. I've never been paddleboarding. I develop a shark phobia if I get too far from shore," I say before pausing. "Just so you know, I didn't think I could be that honest until I wrote mine too. It all kind of just came out. Like, I majorly blogged up."

I did not just say that—not here, not now, not with Dylan right here and now.

"What's 'blogged up'?"

I pause again. I have no choice but to answer. "It's like vomiting but for blogging. Sage and I sort of made it up. I'm sorry—I know that sounds gross."

Dylan laughs and his hair falls over his left eye in the most adorable way. "Hey, just so you know, I'm having a party next Friday. You should come. Sage, too."

Unable to speak, I just nod as Dylan lets go of my arm and leaves the room.

I swear I felt lighter in the water during swim practice. My coach even commended me on my kicking set. Buoyed by both my post and Dylan's party invite, I nearly forgot to worry about what my mom's going to say about my first blog entry.

I almost even forgot that I used the words *blogged up* in front of Dylan.

But the second I get off the bus in front of my house, I feel heavy, not unlike the way I feel the days we have to swim with weights for resistance. I open the door on the side of the garage, and I find Grandma Hope, my dad, and my mom sitting around our kitchen table. This confirms my sinking feeling.

We're not the type for huge family dinners. My grandma likes to do dinner herself; she's big on maintaining her independence *and* watching the Golf Channel while she eats. My mom often spends that time working on her blog, and my dad's not usually home for dinner.

I'm well fed, but we don't do the whole "sit around the table like we're in an old-fashioned Norman Rockwell painting." Of course, on the rare occasions when we do eat together, my mom's sure to take one thousand photos and blog about our perfect family dinner.

People say that a Christmas card shows a lot about how a family *wants* to be seen. Just imagine if, every day, your mom posted images of you and your family. You'd have thousands of visions of what your mom *wants* you and your family to be. But they'd always look like a scrapbook of someone else's life.

"Have a seat," my mom says to me. Grandma Hope shoots her a disapproving look, but my mom doesn't relax a muscle in her face—or in her body. She's as stiff as a taxidermy tarpon.

I pull out a pastel pink chair and sit at our round dinner table, which is constructed entirely from old driftwood. My dad made it for my mom as a wedding gift. Our whole house has a very cool beach-bungalow vibe. Usually it feels homey and airy, but right now it feels tense and tight.

"I read your blog," Mom says slowly.

Obviously, I think.

"Your mom is a bit . . ." My dad pauses and curls his front lip over his teeth. He sighs. "She's been feeling a bit emotional. I think her feelings might have been hurt."

My mom grips the table with one hand as if she were on the teacup ride at Disney World and were trying to stop it from spinning.

"You will delete it. I already emailed your teacher my thoughts on whatever she's 'teaching,'" my mom says. Her voice grows louder as she makes sweeping quotation marks with her fingers.

"Let Imogene speak, Meg," Grandma Hope says, waving her hand at my mom. "Maybe that's what she's doing with this whole thing. Trying to say something."

"Mom, your job is to blog," I say slowly. "My job is to be a student and do well at school. Right now that means I also have a blog. If you let me approve what you post about me on your blog, then I'll grant you the same respect and privilege. What about those unflattering photos from this weekend? Did you even think I just wanted to enjoy Grandma's tournament, not be a cardboard prop for you to move around a golf course?"

My dad, mom, and Grandma Hope all look up at me in surprise. All my life, I've tried to talk to my mom about the blog, but I've never really been so direct about it—until right now.

"How did *I* look in the golf pictures?" my grandma asks with a smirk. She's trying to break the tension, but it isn't working. "I'm hoping you shot only my left side. That's my good one."

"You looked like the ace you are," I say. I need to do everything I can, including sucking up, to keep Grandma Hope on my side.

My dad jumps from his chair and swiftly moves into the kitchen. "Why don't we eat dinner?" He picks up a tray and carries it over to the table. He worked his way through college as a waiter, and it shows. He sets the tray down in front of us. "I marinated chicken breasts in apricot jam. We can talk about this when everyone is less hungry and sensitive. Nobody should ever talk about the big stuff without a full stomach."

No one says a word over dinner. We all quietly eat then wash our own dishes.

Before I go up to my room, my mom stops me and says, "Imogene, you looked very preppy chic in those golf pictures. I don't understand why you're so insecure. You're so beautiful. A lot of the readers have been commenting on how pretty and grown-up you are looking these days."

I don't respond; I know she's just trying to get me to cave in like I always do. It's Mommylicious's way.

But I'm not giving up that easily today. For the first time ever, my mom is finally beginning to know what it feels like to be me.

The Mommy Bloggers' Daughters:
The Girl on That Blog

"Let's Make a Deal"

<u>THIS</u> is a picture of my mom sleeping.
Isn't it cute?
<u>THIS</u> is a picture of my mom eating.
Isn't it cute?
<u>THIS</u> is a picture of my mom blogging.
Triple cute.
That's all for today, folks.
Skulls and Bones,
Don't Dare Call Me Babylicious

The Mommy Bloggers' Daughters: Life with VeggieMom

"I Said I Was Looking at New School Shoes, but I Was Really . . ."

Eating at Panda Express. The lo mein was delish! I could even taste the MSG. My only regret: I wish I had ordered an egg roll.

Then I went to Chick-fil-A. Their biscuits are to die for. I can taste the butter in nearly every bite. Awesome.

Read my mom's post about how fast food is killing our youth HERE. I'm sure she'll be grateful for the page clicks.

Yours Truly,

Fast-FoodBaby!

Mommylicious

"To Ground or Not to Ground?
That Is the Question."

Hello, Readerlicious!

Hope everyone is having a great Friday. I taste tested Welch's new organic fruit snacks and my mouth is still tingling. Totally juicilious. Read my review HERE.

Today, of course, is BIG QUESTION DAY, when I ask a parenting question and give my opinion. In the old days the BIG QUESTIONS were somewhat easier. Breast milk or formula? What's too young for a sleepover? What to do with a chronic bed-wetter? (Luckily, Imogene's grown out of that phase.) Writing about parenting questions has always helped me reflect on how I can be the best mommy I can be.

But as Imogene is getting older, the questions are getting harder and harder to answer. And I'm becoming less and less sure of my own answers. Anyone else out there having a similar experience?

This week's question—To ground or not to ground?—is a tricky one. Recently Imogene crossed some no-no boundaries and she's refusing to a) apologize or b) promise that she won't do it again. I'm not going to go into all the details, but I'm currently deciding (with some help from Daddylicious) whether we're going to ground her for the weekend. Apparently, there's some *big pool party*, so she would definitely be upset. But the question remains: Will she learn her lesson?

What do you readers think? Does grounding work? I can't say I have an answer myself. This is uncharted territory.

Butterfly Kisses,

Mommylicious

PS Look at these delicious chicken breasts Hubby made. Recipe <u>HERE</u>! What a great family dinner we had. Check out <u>THIS</u> family pic. (I think I caught them by surprise! Oops! Next time I'll remember to say cheese.)

Chapter Seven

THE ARMISTICE

IT'S NEVER A GOOD THING TO HAVE TO STAY AFTER CLASS, BUT it's Shakespearean-level tragic when it's the last period on a Friday and there's a pool party in four hours. A pool party that your moms are threatening to ground you from going to because you keep blogging about them. A pool party that you must go to because your crush will be there, and you want him to ask you to the Pirate's Booty Ball more than anything—except maybe getting your mom to stop blogging about you.

Once the other students leave the classroom, Ms. Herring closes the door behind them and sits at her desk. "Girls, your last posts were . . . *interesting*."

In the eighth grade, our English teacher instructed us to never use the word *interesting*. She said it's hollow and vague. After hearing Ms. Herring say it, I have to agree with her. It's also scary.

"Thanks, I'm glad that you liked them," Sage says. She taps her fingers on Ms. Herring's desk.

Sometimes I catch Sage pretending to play the piano on any surface she can find. Her desk. The lunch table. A car's dashboard. I tease her that she probably does it in her sleep, too. She's as passionate about it as her mom is about being vegan.

Ms. Herring sighs deeply. "I wasn't using the word *interesting* as a compliment, Sage. While I think it was very brave of you two to make your blogs public and to write about a topic that is personal to you, your last few posts have been devoid of any real subject or service. I was a little worried about the tone in the first posts, but I think my excitement over the project took over and I might have encouraged you girls in the wrong direction. I apologize if I did. I want you to know that these recent posts went in a different direction from what originally I intended for this project."

She doesn't say it in a mean voice, but there's an adult tone to it. It's definitely not the same voice she uses when she mentions *So You Think You Can Dance?*

If these blogs are supposed to be about our lives, shouldn't they reflect how we feel? Why do we have to change our tone if it's genuine to our feelings?

Ms. Herring purses her lips.

"I'm worried that you girls are using these blogs to attack your mothers and their blogs rather than write about your *own* lives," she adds.

Now I want to scream. Our lives and our mothers' blogs are tangled like knots. Our lives *are* their blogs. Instead I ask calmly, "Are you a blog reader?"

The clock is ticking, and I need to make sure this meeting doesn't last any longer than it needs to.

"I do read quite a few blogs," she says. "I've even been thinking of starting my own."

Of course, everyone *and* their goldfish are thinking about starting a blog. Everyone except for me and Sage . . . until now.

"Do all the blogs you read have a clear subject or a service?" I ask.

"Most do," she says after a pause.

Sage leans over Ms. Herring's desk. "But many don't, right? Many are just pictures of their kids looking cute or food diaries or other pointless junk. So what you're really saying is that you don't want us to write an honest blog. You want us to write something entirely different."

"I want to read something that matters to you—not something that you're writing just to bother your moms," Ms. Herring says. "That said, I support protecting freedom of speech, and I won't stand for the banning of a book—or a blog. Please know that I'm not censoring you two in any way, but I did promise your mothers that I'd speak with you. As I'm sure you both know, they are very upset."

"Thank you for your concern," Sage says, shifting her body weight back. "These posts do matter to us and we're not doing them *just* to bother our moms. But we heard what you just said too and we'll talk with our moms. We promise."

Sage gives Ms. Herring a sympathetic look while she picks up her book bag and waits for her to say it's okay for us to leave. Finally Ms. Herring gives us a defeated wave and says, "Have a nice weekend."

"You too," I say on my way out. I feel badly that Ms. Herring has gotten wrapped up in the Mommy Bloggers' Daughters. But I still feel better having put my thoughts out there. No one's teased me about my mom's blog since the Mommy Bloggers' Daughters went viral.

Sage and I wait near the tennis courts for my mom to pick us up. Last night my mom announced that we'd be having a powwow with Sage and her mom about our blogs. "To discuss whatever is going on in your heads." My mom's words, not mine.

At my dad's and grandmother's requests, our blogging powwow is being held at the beach.

Grandma Hope specifically said, "We're not getting

involved. Please don't bring these internet fights into the home. We have to have *some* separation between the real world and the Bermuda Blog Triangle."

"You know that I don't like it when you call it that. It's called the internet. You should try it someday. It's pretty mind-blowing," my mom said. "I know it's not *golf*, but a lot of people are rather jazzed about it, since it changed the world and all."

"Yes, please have the meeting outside of the house," my dad said, and Grandma nodded in support. Even though my grandma Hope is my dad's mother-in-law, they get along famously. My grandma actually met my dad first when he caddied for her. "He had the best eye of them all," she says about my dad's caddying skills. "I wanted my daughter to be with someone who knew golf that well. Golf is about more than just playing the game, you know."

I spot my mom's station wagon pulling into the school's parking lot; the decal is hard to miss. Sage and I get into the backseat, and we silently drive the few blocks to the beach.

The best part of living in a seasonal community is that there are a few months when the beach is finally just for locals. Late September is hurricane season, and it's also before the Snowbirds land. (Snowbirds are people, mostly very old people, who live in Florida for about six months of the year to escape northern winters.) Today's one of those rare and precious times that the beach is empty and free of little kids and Snowbirds, who hog every inch of the sand during the busy season. While it's great that it's beautiful and peaceful, it might be nice to have a few witnesses on this deserted beach in case things get out of hand.

Ms. Carter is already sitting on a rainbow-colored beach towel when we enter the beach from the sandy public access path. She's wearing a blue tie-dye maxi skirt and a spaghetti-strapped white tank top. My mom calls Ms. Carter's look "boho chic," but Sage and I call it "Hippie: Version Twenty-First Century."

As we approach, Ms. Carter's giving Sage the same look my mom's been giving me all week. It's the "Do I know you? Where'd my daughter go?" look.

My mom unfolds a checkered beach blanket and spreads it out on the sand. From a cooler bag, Ms. Carter pulls out three small Tupperware containers, one with carrot sticks, one with celery stalks, and one with cherry tomatoes. I wish that my mom was in charge of snacks, especially when I realize there's no dip or peanut butter. Just straight-up vegetables. No wonder Sage is ready for the Mommy Bloggers' Daughters. Isn't part of being a teenager getting to eat junk food while your metabolism is still working?

We all sit down. With my mom and Ms. Carter on her towel, and Sage and me on the beach blanket across from them, the battle lines have been drawn.

"Imogene, Sage," my mom says. "We need to set some boundaries here. We've both been very hurt by your blog posts. To be honest, we feel antagonized. You're making us look like villains. What would our followers think? I know that the Mommylicionados would be pretty disappointed by this if they stumbled upon your blog. This isn't the Babylicious they know and love."

Maybe it isn't Babylicious, but it's Imogene. And I don't even know how my mom uses the word *Mommylicianados* without cracking up.

"I agree," Ms. Carter says. "I'm trying to start a food revolution, but meanwhile, my own daughter is writing about how she's singlehandedly keeping our mall's food court in business. It sends very mixed messages."

Neither Sage nor I speak. I bury my feet in the sand and look out to the horizon while Sage plays the piano on the Tupperware.

"Are these boundaries going to apply to both moms *and* daughters?" Sage finally asks. "Like, if *you* say no photos, then do we *all* stop with the photos—or just us? Because if it's just us, that's not fair."

Ms. Carter guides Sage's fingers off the Tupperware. "Sage! Our blogs are our businesses. They put food on the table. It's a little different from some silly school project."

I underhand toss a carrot to a seagull. I breathe in

deeply. "Do you guys *really* think that this is about a *silly* school project?" Like, do we need to bring in a psychiatrist to tell you what this is about? I add in my head, but not out loud. My blog has opened my floodgates, but only so far.

Neither of our moms responds.

"All we're doing is what you guys have been always doing: We're writing about our lives and the people in our lives," Sage argues. She takes my lead and throws a celery stick at the same seagull. Her mom gives her a look: "What, Mom? I'm just trying to give the bird some healthy food. All the tourists probably poisoned it this summer with potato chips."

Ms. Carter glares at Sage.

"Here's the deal, girls. We might all be bloggers now, but we're still the mothers. We're still in charge," my mom's voice booms. She's totally using her "conference voice," which is this super-confident "Mommy-power ra-ra-ra" voice that she puts on anytime she's asked to speak to bloggers or blog readers. It's part of her persona. It's her *voice-ilicous.*

"Do we need to remind you girls that you're only fifteen years old? We have decades more of life than you two. Trust us that we know what's best."

"Meg's right," Ms. Carter agrees. "We already discussed all of this earlier. We're not having a *conversation* about guidelines. We're *informing* you two of the guidelines. From now on, we'll need to approve *every* post. The posts will not be negative in subject or tone. If we didn't approve a post and we find it online, you'll delete it and be grounded for a month. We don't want this school project to jeopardize you girls' future."

Sage stands up and points at her mom. "You mean *your* future, Mom. I imagine that this *discussion* is over since all it turned out to be was a lecture about more elements of my life that you want to control."

I stand up with my friend. "I suppose that the pool party isn't happening?" I think about how this has probably ruined my one chance to see Dylan and his house.

My mom smiles and her scowl softens. "No, you both can still go. After much thought and some helpful feedback from readers, we've decided not to ground you after all. See, we're not total momsters."

Then my mom reaches for her purse and pulls out her iPhone. *Tap, tap, tap* go her fingers on the screen.

She's either Tweeting or composing a note on what she'll blog about this later. After anything important—or even unimportant—happens, my mom's always on her phone immediately after, updating her following.

Click, click, click goes the camera.

I rarely even notice anymore, but today it all boils my blood. I notice that Ms. Carter is also searching for her phone.

"Mom, I'll check out your post later to see how you felt this went," I say calmly even though my insides are roasting. "Or you could Tweet me," I add even though I do not have—and will never get—a Twitter account. Believe me, when you have a mom who Tweets, that's more than enough chirping for one household.

My mom doesn't reply. She doesn't even look up from her iPhone.

Chapter Eight

THE NEW BLOGS ON THE BLOCK

SAGE AND I AGREE TO MEET ON GORDON STREET, ONE OF THE roads that run parallel to the Gulf of Mexico. We're going to walk together over to Dylan's house for the pool party. After today's smackdown with the mommy bloggers, I'm not feeling nearly as thrilled about the party as I was only four hours ago.

If we blog about what we want to, we're grounded. If we *don't* blog about what we want to, we've given up on our mission, and everything goes back to how it was.

It's been less than two weeks, and I feel like I've failed already.

Sage is sitting under the shade of a palm tree when I walk up to her. Although she doesn't listen to her mom about much, she is super-vigilant about the sun, even at five o'clock in the evening. "We're originally from Minnesota," she explains. "I'm a descendent of the Vikings—and the Chinese, but mostly the Vikings. My skin is not used to eighty-seven degrees when it's almost October."

Sage's wearing a black cover-up and purple flip-flops, and I can see through her sheer cover-up that she went with her one-piece swimsuit. At the last minute, I ditched my red halter one-piece for a two-piece tropical-print string bikini from Tommy Bahama. I pull down on my yellow sundress.

"Going for the bikini!" Sage catcalls. "Hot. You're working hard on Pirate's Booty Ball already. Stop blushing. You look great. Dylan's going to die."

"*Shhh*. Someone might overhear you," I squeal.

Sage motions around to the empty street and laughs. She pretends to play the piano and belts out "Your Song" by Elton John. That's how good Sage is at music. She's only fifteen and she can do Elton.

"Dylan thinks of me as Babylicious, just like everyone else," I say. "I'm that girl on the blog."

"And I'm the girl whose mom brought tofu cakes in every year for her birthday. In an eight-year-old's world, that's similar to treason. If I lived in pirate times, I definitely would've walked the plank. Do you know that people *still* tease me about that? But, Imogene, you know that we're more than the sum of our mom's blogs. Isn't that what we're working to show with the Mommy Bloggers' Daughters?"

I nod. Sage's right. Just like everyone else, we're more than who our moms portray us to be. We're growing up, and they don't own us.

That's what the Mommy Bloggers' Daughters is about, I remind myself. I start to feel renewed about our mission, despite the grounding threat that looms over us. Besides, all change has a cost, and maybe I'm finally willing to pay the price for my freedom. Or at least, I think I am. I've never actually been grounded, so I'm guessing here.

We follow the pedestrian lane down a banyan-tree-lined street. To the west, we can see the ocean, where the sky's turned a mix of pink and periwinkle, and the sun is slowly making its way to bed. That's how my dad always describes it, and I love the expression.

"This is the maddest I've ever been at my mom," Sage says.

We move out of the way of a biker coming down the pedestrian path.

"The maddest ever?" I ask. For me, that was definitely when my mom posted about my first period or about how I felt horrible about failing an algebra test. A forty-two out of one hundred. (I'm okay with numbers, but once letters get into the math mix, I'm gone-zo.)

I spot across the street one of the first houses my dad designed. It's a Tuscan-style mini-mansion, and every detail is beautiful, from the arched doorways to its terra-cotta roof. Some of my favorite memories with my dad are driving around Naples and seeing the homes he designed. We should do that again soon, because it's been a really long time. Maybe that'd cheer him up and make him feel good about his work again.

Sage stops suddenly. "I'm furious," she says. "They aren't letting us write about our lives, even though they've been writing about us since forever. My mom decides my life down to every morsel of food that I eat, and then she blogs about it on top of that. How come I can't do the same? What happened to freedom of speech?"

Sage pauses. "Does it only apply to her? She might as well just burn my computer like the Nazis did with books they didn't like. I actually thought my blog would be a wake-up call to her, but it hasn't been at all. It's just some-thing else she wants to control for me. Aren't you *mad*?"

We cross the street and enter into Dylan's posh Port Royal neighborhood. I point in the direction of Dylan's house. "Of course I'm angry, Sage. But let's not think about it right now," I say. I squeeze Sage's hand. "For the party, let's just be normal."

"You're right," she agrees, and pulls me up Dylan's brick driveway. "I'll forget it for the night. Or I'll try to. Let's work on getting some Pirate's Booty Ball dates."

Dylan's mom answers the door. She's one of those "I

can't believe she's a mom" moms. She's wearing a Tory Burch tunic that's borderline dress, borderline shirt, and three-inch straw platforms. Dylan definitely inherited his good looks from her.

"Hello, girls," she says, putting in a starfish earring. "I'm just heading out to an event. But just so you know, Luz, our housekeeper, is supervising, and I hired a lifeguard. You can never be too careful."

She points at a caterer, who's balancing a tray of lemonades in champagne glasses. "Take one. They're mocktails. Our caterer, You've Got It Coming, thinks of just about everything."

"Thank you, Mrs. Mulberry," I say.

"You're welcome, Imogene," she says. I don't think we've ever officially met, but I can guess how she knows my name. At least she didn't call me Babylicious.

While Sage and I chime our glasses and take small sips, Mrs. Mulberry slips out through the front door.

I knew that Dylan lived in a fancy neighborhood, but I had no idea that his house was a mansion. Or that they had a *staff.* He comes across as so down-to-earth.

How amazing would it be to *not* have your mom bothering you all the time? His mom knows that he's having a party, and she doesn't even stay. She actually treats him like a grown-up. If I ever had a party, my mom would hover like a helicopter and snap photographs as if Kate Middleton were the guest of honor. One reason I stopped having birthday parties after I turned ten.

Through the glass living room doors, I can see some of our classmates already cannonballing into the infinity pool. Others are gathered around an outdoor TV on the lanai—that's the Florida word for an outside living room. Football highlights are playing on the TV, and the boys are hollering at the Gators. Most of the girls are relaxing on chaise lounges around the pool.

As soon as Sage and I step out onto the patio, Mackenzie Miller, Anne Roberts, and Sara Cho are on their feet and moving toward us.

"Omigosh!" Mackenzie screeches. "We didn't think you'd show. Someone told us that y'all got grounded for all of October because your moms are so furious. You guys' posts were, like, so honest. It was scary crazy. Y'all are taking on the establishment and putting the fight online."

They usher us to a corner of the pool with thronelike outdoor furniture with blue padding. "Please sit down and tell us everything," Anne says.

Sage and I look at each other, puzzled, but we both plop down as the other girls continue to hover around us. I try to spot Dylan in the sea of guys near the TV, but I don't see him.

"I heard that your mom is *suing* the school over Ms. Herring's assignment," Sara says, looking at me. "Fiction or fact?"

"We're not grounded . . . yet, and Imogene's mom is not suing the school," Sage says. "But, yes, our moms are mad, that part is totally correct."

"My mom says that it's only fair after all the details your moms put online about you two," Mackenzie says. "No offense or anything. That's just her opinion."

"None taken," I say as I try to adjust to this scene. Sage and I have never been the center of anything other than teasing about our mom's blogs. All of a sudden, it seems as if we're almost popular.

"Can one of you do me a favor?" Sara asks. "Can you get my mom to stop posting about me on Facebook? Maybe you could write a blog entry about how annoying that is? Can you believe that she actually tried to friend Dylan Mulberry? The woman has no boundaries," Sara says, sighing. She points at herself. "*I'm* not even friends with him. It's also just plain creepy for an adult woman to friend a teen boy on Facebook. She's going to accidentally end up on *To Catch a Predator* if she's not more careful."

For a second, I wish I were still on Facebook so I could be friends with Dylan. But my mom wouldn't let me be on it unless I was her friend, and I couldn't stand her constant Mommylicious—and Babylicious—updates. I'm totally with Sara. You aren't actually "friends" with your kids' friends, so you shouldn't friend them on Facebook.

"That's not a bad idea about the blog post," Sage says to Anne. "Maybe I'll do my next post on parents and Facebook. Mark Zuckerberg has created a monster. I want to start a new social network, where no parents or adults are allowed."

Sage is dreaming up a new teenager-only social media site when I see Dylan walking around near the other side of the pool.

"Thanks for having us, Dylan," I call out, trying not to sound too eager.

He gives a brief wave before going the few steps to watch TV in the lanai. I only wish Dylan found me as interesting as Mackenzie, Sara, and Anne do right now.

"Well, we're going to get more mocktails," Anne announces. "I've had two already and have a total sugar buzz going on. But, just so you know, I think it's awesome what you guys are doing." She flips her long blond hair, and it cascades over her tangerine sundress. "You guys are somehow making homework cool *and* going up against your parents. Everyone's talking about it."

From near the diving board, I spot Ardsley and her shadow, Tara Bennett, watching Sage and me in the middle of the group. Apparently, Anne's right. Everyone, including Ardsley, is paying attention to us. It feels nice to finally be noticed for something other than being Baby-licious.

Bing, chimes my phone. Again.

Mom: I'm coming to pick you up in 10 minutes. Stop ignoring my texts. 10-4.

I sigh because the party's just getting fun.

Everyone keeps asking about our blogs *and* Katy Perry's blasting on the outdoor speakers *and* Luz just put out an ice cream sundae bar *and* I almost have the courage to talk to Dylan, who's spent most of his own party being quiet and watching TV.

"My mom's coming in ten," I whisper to Sage. "She never lets me have any fun."

Sage licks her ice cream to prevent it from melting. She was all over the sundae bar.

"Do you mind if I catch a ride?" Sage asks. "I need to practice piano, and I want to work on my blog, too."

"Wow," I say. "You're being super-serious. I was just going to watch TV and go to bed."

"Imogene," she says, pointing her cone at me. "You should work on your blog too! After all, the Mommy Bloggers' Daughters was *your* idea. You're not all of a sudden bowing out just because our moms threatened to ground us, are you?"

94

I don't answer her right away. I want more than anything for my mom to stop blogging about me, but I also don't want to be grounded. The point of all this is for us to have a normal life. But Sage is right. I can't give in *this* easily.

"I'm in. I'm in," I say. "Don't worry, Sage. Be right back," I say, standing up to find Dylan.

I spot him sitting on a chair alone near the TV. I've gone to school with Dylan since forever, but I don't really know him. I don't think anyone does. He's popular with everyone, yet doesn't have any close friends—or a girl-friend.

"Hey, Dylan," I say, making my way toward him. "Thanks for the great party. My mom's picking me up, and she won't take no for an answer, otherwise I'd stay longer."

"That's nice of her," he says, looking up at me.

"Trust me," I say. "You wouldn't want my mom. Your mom has a life. My mom has a blog."

"I think you're too hard on her," Dylan says. He looks away from me back to the TV.

"Excuse me—" I start to say just as Sage yells, "Imogene, your mom's here!"

In the distance, I can hear Ardsley calling, "Babylicious, Mommylicious is here!" but I don't even care. All I care about is that Dylan and I are having a conversation—maybe even the beginning of an argument—and I have to leave.

Does Dylan read my blog outside of the time Ms. Herring showed it to everyone? And if he does, what does that mean? Why does he think I'm too hard on her? He doesn't know me.

I turn to head toward the sliding doors to the kitchen as I try to figure out what he just meant by that. Before I walk away, I softly say, "I'm not too hard on her. It's complicated."

"Just my opinion," Dylan says, waving his hand as if to say, "No big deal." "No hard feelings. Thanks for coming, Imogene."

Sage raises her eyebrows at me as we make our way through the house and out the front door to my mom's car.

Just as I'm opening the door to the backseat to get in, my mom snaps a picture of me on her phone. I can usually guess which pictures I end up looking cross-eyed in, and that definitely was one of them. Awesome.

"So cute!" she says. "My baby after a pool party. You aren't blushing, are you, Imogene? Is there some boy you like? Was there a good-night kiss?"

Sage stifles a laugh, and I nudge her in the ribs.

"It's not funny," I say to Sage. "And, Mom, by the way, I wanted to let you know that everyone *loves* my blog. Sage's, too. We already have a major following. In fact, I think I'm even starting to understand what it's like to be a blog celebrity like you."

My mom purses her lips, turns around, and starts the car.

The Mommy Bloggers' Daughters is so on.

Mommylicious

"How to Deal"

Dear Readers,

Thanks for all your advice about setting boundaries and outlining consequences. I think that I finally got through to Imogene, aka Babylicious. Three cheers for all the moms out there with teenagers. We definitely deserve Nobel Peace Prizes. Keep up the hard work.

In other news, Imogene went to the pool party. And she wore a two-piece!!! ☺ By the way, she's going to review Roxy's collection soon. Thanks, Roxy. ☺ Dig This Life.

I definitely think there's a boy in Imogene's life. All the telltale signs are there: spending extra time getting ready, blushing, daydreaming, being short with her mother. To be honest, I'm not sure that I'm ready yet for her to have a boyfriend.

Mommies out there, isn't it hard letting your kids grow up? How do you give your kids space but still feel like you know them? One day you're the center of their world; the next they don't even want you to be seen with them. What's a good mommy to do?

In other news, next weekend I'll be giving a

Mom-to-Mom talk at the Women's League of Orlando on "Creating and Sustaining Your Own Online Business." Tickets are fifty dollars apiece, and I promise to hand out some never-been-told-before parenting and blogging gems! <u>GET THE TICKETS</u> while they're hot!

Butterfly kisses,

Mommylicious

The Mommy Bloggers' Daughters: The Girl on That Blog

"Babylicious Can Give Tips Too!"

Mommylicious Parenting Tip #17

"Give children choices. Kids like to feel as if they at least have a choice in the matter. Yes, they must get clean. But let them choose between a bath and a shower. Yes, they must go to sleep, but let them choose the bedtime story. I promise giving kids choices leads to having happy children." —Advice from MommyliciousMeg.com

I guess this doesn't apply to teenagers, huh? When's the last time I had a choice about anything?

For example, was I asked if I *wanted* to fly across the country to attend a blogging conference? Nope.com.

Babylicious Truth #1

Just because Mommylicious gives advice, doesn't mean she follows it. Do as she says, not as she does.

And even if the consequence of blogging the truth is being grounded, I'm
still going to blog.
Skulls and Bones,
Don't Dare Call Me Babylicious

The Mommy Bloggers' Daughters: Life with VeggieMom

"The Absolutely True Confessions of a Junk-Food Baby"

My mom says if I blog again and she doesn't like it, I'm grounded. Most days, life with my mom already feels like prison, so I don't think being grounded will feel that different. I already know one thing: This jail's food sucks!

And . . . at the pool party, I ate one ice cream cone, which was definitely not organic. I also ate seventeen maraschino cherries, which are definitely not in season. Ever.

Truly Yours,

VeggieBaby Fights Back

PS Mom, I don't like your homemade tofu. I lied. Repeatedly.

Chapter Nine

TREASURE HUNTING

AT LUNCH ON MONDAY, SAGE AND I SIT WITH ANNE AND Mackenzie, who make us feel like total superheroes (their words, not ours) for continuing with the Mommy Bloggers' Daughters.

"We'd for sure make plans with y'all for this weekend," Anne said. "That is, if you both weren't going to get grounded for life tonight."

It's amazing how simply writing something online equals instant popularity points. I wonder if this is how little kids feel after they make a cool YouTube video and, a week later, are in Los Angeles taping *The Ellen DeGeneres Show*.

Some kids from the sixth grade, who aren't even on my radar, pointed at me in the hallway and one whispered audibly: "That's the girl from the mommy blog, but now she, like, has her own blog about her mom. It's totally a mom-daughter blog war."

The Mommy Bloggers' Daughters posts have even spread to the lower grades. And a blog war? I kind of like the way that sounds.

Very twenty-first century.

Also, Dylan waved hi to me as he walked into English class. So other than it potentially being my last day of freedom, Monday has actually been pretty great.

But as soon as I walk in the front door after swim practice, I hear my mom call out "Im-o-gene." Whenever she goes long on the *O*, I know that I'm in for it.

I follow her voice, and I find her sitting in an armchair in our living room, which is strange since, like most normal people, we rarely spend any time in our living room. We go into ours only for video house tours (it's a blog thing—don't even get me started), and for my mom's annual Christmas blogtail party.

My mom points at a matching armchair. "Sit down."

Sinking into it, I remember why no one actually hangs out in living rooms. They're formal and uncomfortable, all about showing rather than about living.

"First of all, and this goes without saying, you're grounded," my mom says. "Your last post was just mean, Imogene. I can't have my own child mock me on the internet. If you're so angry with me, why don't you just talk to me about it?"

I laugh. I tried hard not to, but if I didn't let this laugh out, I would've choked on it. I cross my legs, trying to get into a sort of comfortable position.

"If you think I have a boyfriend, why don't you just *ask* me instead of writing about it on the internet? By the way, I *so* do not and probably never will because of you and your blog."

I rest my head on my hand and breathe in. I look at my mom. "And now, all of a sudden, *you're* wondering why *I* don't just talk to you instead of writing something on the internet. That's how you communicate, Mom. It's how you've communicated for a *long* time. I'm just following your lead."

I can't believe I said what I just said. I've never spoken to her like this.

My mom shifts her weight in her chair and pauses. I'm hoping it's a life-altering pause that means she finally gets what I've been trying to tell her.

"Imogene, I know that the teen years are rough and that you're going through an independent phase. I'm trying to understand, but I absolutely can't allow you to jeopardize my career and the website that I've built from the ground up. Do you know how many unique visitors I have every day? If my own daughter is writing terrible things about me on the internet and someone finds them, how does that make *me* look? Trust me, I have plenty of enemies online, but I can't allow my daughter to be one of them. I want you to think about what this means for someone other than yourself," she says.

She stands up, then pauses to rub at the Oriental rug with her toes. "You're grounded until I say you're not anymore. You will apologize to me, and then you will delete all the posts I say. Also, if you continue blogging publicly for your class, I will need to preapprove each post, Imogene. I'm not having my career ruined over a school project."

I should've known that pause meant that she didn't get it. She's never "gotten" it. Not the time that she missed my swim championship for a blogging networking event. Not the time that I insisted she not write about a big fight that Sage and I had and she still did. Not ever.

Now I'm grounded because I told her how I feel, and she still doesn't get it. She cares more about her PR than me. It's always how it looks and never how it is—just like this living room. What I want to say to my mom is, *Where's your apology? The one where you ask me to forgive you for turning me and my life into a blog?*

She's worried about her *career*. Well, Mom, I'm worried about my life, which I think is a little more important than your career.

My mom leaves the room, and I just sit, dazed at how

moms can be so clueless, especially mine, a self-professed mommy expert.

I feel my phone vibrating in my backpack, and I pull it out.

Sage: Grounded indefinitely. Total bloodbath over here.
Me: Me too.
Sage: I know it's worth it still. See you tomorrow.

Throughout the week, the rumors circulating about the Mommy Bloggers' Daughters churn like a tropical storm that's gaining force. Even *Ardsley* asked me if it was true that my mom took away my computer and donated it to Goodwill. Totally false, but I'm happy that Ardsley's actually talking to me rather than just teasing me. Modest progress.

Somehow, although I'm grounded and my mom can't stand to look at me, I feel better than I have in a long time.

Fortunately, it's also finally Friday, and my mom's going to Orlando for a blogging event. Of course, I'm still on house arrest, but at least I'll be free of her.

"I'm home," I call out after swim practice on Friday. "Did Mom leave my ball and chain?"

To my surprise, when I walk into the house, I find both my grandma and my dad sitting on the couch together.

"No golf today? I thought Friday was your most lucky

day." I plop my tote bag down on a leather chair.

Grandma Hope always plays Friday afternoons with her friends. They call it their Friday Fun in the Sun Club.

Grandma Hope points to her left wrist, which is wrapped in an Ace bandage. "Georgia, honey, I'm in the reserves now."

"Oh my God. What happened?" I exclaim. "Are you okay?"

"It was on the fifth hole," Grandma Hope says, squinting her eyes. "That's our par three, and I always hook it just a little. But today I overcompensated and I sliced it, and it ended up lying awkwardly near a banyan tree root. I went to chip it in and *bam*! Heavens! I've always hated that hole."

"English, not Golf-speak, Grandma," I say. "What did the doctor say? Are you all right?"

In my whole life, my grandma's practically never complained about a headache. When she came to live with us, she even insisted on helping the movers carry boxes. Her motto is "I'll catch up on rest when I'm dead."

"No, I'm *not* okay," Grandma Hope says breathlessly. "I can't play golf for *four* weeks. Can you believe that, Georgia? I'm not even allowed to putt, not even that silly mini putt-putt with windmills, waterfalls, bridges, trolls, and whatnot. I asked about *that* because I was flat desperate. I've never had to take this much time off from golf, not even when your mom was born. I had her—she was nine pounds, three ounces, I might add—and I still shot a seventy-five three weeks later."

I look at my dad. He nods at me.

"Hope's going to be fine. It's a sprain," he translates.

I sigh in relief and plop down on the couch.

"Well, at least, she'll be physically okay. Mentally . . . I'm not so sure," he adds.

"If you weren't my favorite son-in-law . . ." Grandma Hope gently whacks Dad with her good hand.

My dad shrugs. "I'm your *only* son-in-law."

"Exactly," Grandma Hope says.

My mom is an only child. Grandma Hope always says, "My other kid is golf, and luckily, I always know my score with that one and I even get a handicap to boot. Wish it were that easy with your mother."

Grandma Hope takes the remote from my dad and programs it to channel 723, the Golf Channel. "I guess I'll just have to watch other people play golf for a month, which is like forcing a dieting woman to watch Paula Deen cook meat loaf and bake pies. It's just flat-out cruel."

"I'm indefinitely grounded too, Grandma Hope," I say. "We can be shut-ins together. Did Mom still leave for Orlando?"

"Yes," Grandma Hope says. She pushes her fingers under the bandage and massages her wrist. "She took me to the hospital and then dropped me off at home before she headed out. She got a few pictures first. . . . Hey, Georgia, when are you two going to figure this thing out? This house is turning into a skating pond with all the thin ice around here. Now we're all trapped together, and I can't even escape to the golf course."

I cozy up on the couch between my dad and Grandma Hope. "I'm sorry, Grandma Hope. But I think that my blog is important, and I might finally be getting somewhere, even if I'm technically not *going* anywhere, since I'm grounded."

"Well, that's good that you think it's working," Grandma Hope says. "I have a rule about not reading *anyone's* blog. I read your mom's once—and believe me, that didn't end a million miles near good. Don't worry, I'm not going to read yours. It's such a blessing that I don't know how to use the internet."

My dad coughs loudly. "Excuse me, what about me?" my dad asks. "Do I have to be stuck here on a beautiful Friday night with you two prisoners? I hope you realize that people work their butts off for their entire lives to retire to Florida. And what are we doing?" He points at at the TV. "We're watching old fogies hit a tiny white ball and wasting our good fortune of calling Florida our home. We're almost as bad as *your mother,*" he says to me, "and *your daughter,*" he says to Grandma Hope, "who spends her entire life behind a computer screen."

"I can't," I answer. I put my hands behind my back like I'm being handcuffed. "I'm grounded, remember."

My dad rolls his eyes at me. He takes my grandma's good arm and pulls her up off the couch.

"You're allowed to go on a walk with your family, Imogene. Personally, I hope you two quit this nonsense soon. I just want a happy family. Is that too much for a man to ask? This place is one combustible ball of estrogen."

I begin to feel guilty again that my dad's stuck in the middle of all this.

Grandma Hope shakes her head. "We have to let Georgia make her own decisions, but I'm hoping this all ends soon too. Otherwise, I'm going to need some ice skates," she says. "At least you can skate just fine with a bum wrist."

While I'm laughing at the idea of my grandma skating around our kitchen, I watch my dad check the grandfather clock and then pluck his iPad off the kitchen counter.

"We still have that app for the tides, right?" he asks while swiping away at his iPad. I notice his fingers are covered in ink, which is a telltale sign he's been working on blueprints today.

"Perfect," he says, lighting up more than I've seen since he told me about the development going to another firm. "Low tide. It's beachcombing time."

My dad is, well . . . he used to be, very serious about

beachcombing. Thankfully, he doesn't use a metal detector and look for buried treasure or anything lame like that. Typically, he collects things that people have left, and also items the ocean has returned to the shore. Once, he found an actual message in a bottle. He doesn't go that often anymore because of work, but when I was a little girl, we used to go all the time.

"How about a round of golf instead?" Grandma Hope asks. "My wrist miraculously feels better already. Doctors today don't know squat. They all just got into it because of that doctor soap opera. I watched that show once. All sex, no medicine. My doctor was probably too busy thinking about sex and he didn't realize that my wrist is totally fine."

I see my dad shiver dramatically each time my grandma mentions sex, but he keeps heading toward the closet near the pantry. He opens it and grabs a small shovel and a plastic laundry basket.

Grandma Hope gives my dad a onceover look and shakes her head. "Sand is the golfer's enemy," she says. "Why would I want to electively go spend time in what I view as the largest sand trap out there?"

"Hope," my dad says firmly, pointing his nearly blue finger at her. "I need a distraction from work, and pretty soon Imogene is going to be a high-schooler with no time for us. Think of this like we're going treasure hunting.

Florida has more to it than golf, and the ocean was here long before the golf courses were. We can survive without golf, but not without water."

"Speak for yourself, son. This 'no golf' thing might just kill me, but okay, okay, I'll go," she agrees. "Just know that you can't teach an old dog new tricks, so I'm warning you that I'll probably be grumpy. And if my wrist hurts, we're calling it a day and going for ice cream."

The three of us pile into the Wagoneer and head for the beach near the Naples pier. Once we get there, Grandma Hope and I quickly follow after my dad's sand footprints, just trying to keep up with his brisk pace.

Immediately my dad finds a Nerf football.

"Awesome," he says. He spikes it into the basket. "Now, Imogene, if I see something good out in the water, you have to be my retriever."

"Okay," I say, happy to make him happy. "It's a good thing that I'm on the swim team."

Often at low tide, objects will be brought back toward the beach, and we'll see them floating in waves. A retriever is the person who swims out to get those items. The best times of all to beachcomb are the days right after a big storm like Hurricane Wilma.

"Georgia! I see something sticking out over there. Start digging. I'm injured," Grandma Hope says.

Her voice sounds almost excited, so I get on my hands

and knees, start to dig, and pull out a pair of kids' cat-eyed sunglasses.

"Very cool," she says. "The only free things on the golf course are rogue golf balls and broken tees. Maybe I *should* get off the golf course more often."

"Please, Grandma Hope, you'll be back on the golf course the day the doctor gives the okay. Or the day before," I say.

I hand the sunglasses to my grandma, who dusts them off and squeezes them on, which makes my dad laugh. This would be a photo op for my mom, and we'd all have to stop to take a bunch of pictures.

I know it's wrong, but I'm glad that she's not here. Yet, I still keep looking around for a camera. I wonder if this is the same feeling people get the first few days after leaving a reality show.

Out on the water, past the first few sets of breaking waves, I spot a paddleboarder riding the Gulf's small swells. He's using his paddle as a rudder behind him. After a closer look, I realize it's not just any paddleboarder—it's Dylan. I should've guessed that I'd run into him since he lives near the beach, and we're walking right by the Port Royal Club, a fancy private beach club for just his neighborhood.

Please don't let him see me.

Grandma Hope catches my stare. "What a cute young boy! I wish that they had paddleboarding back in my day. Maybe I'll pick that up in my nineties. They say it's a great abdominal workout, and I'm always looking for a way to get into that itsy bitsy, teeny weeny, yellow polka-dot bikini."

I know that my grandma's only joking, as she's firmly against bikinis of all kinds. "Goodness. Let's leave *something*, even if it's just a belly button, up to the imagination," she always says when she sees me in one.

Like a puppy retrieving a tennis ball, my dad brings over his newest treasure, a dolphin-shaped sand toy.

He notices us looking out to the ocean and he blocks the setting sun with his hand so he can peer out too.

"Hey, isn't that your classmate Dylan?" my dad asks. "He's had that blond curly hair since kindergarten. Why don't you say hi?"

My dad begins to wave and I pull his arm down.

"No, thanks, Dad," I say quickly. "He's obviously busy. We're not even really friends. We just have a couple of classes together."

I turn my back toward the ocean and start walking. I hope Grandma Hope and Dad will follow my lead.

"Does someone have a crush?" Grandma Hope asks. "I've heard your mom yapping about that possibility, and now it looks like we've found him. You're blushing sun-burn red, Georgia. Hey, I have an idea: Let's invite him over for dinner."

"Are you sure you didn't injure your head along with your wrist?" I hiss.

I take a few steps along the beach and then glare at my grandma and Dad, who are still gawking like seagulls at Dylan.

"I'm serious. Please keep moving," I say, but it's already too late. Dylan's riding a wave all the way in, and he has already spotted us.

"Imogene, hi!" he says. He jumps off his paddleboard and drags it up past the tide.

"Hi, Dylan," I say. "You looked like you were having fun out there. Sorry to run, but we're heading back to the pier. See y-you Monday," I manage to stammer out.

Dylan steps in front of our path.

He points at our basket. "What'd you all find?" Dylan asks.

"Junk," I say. "Nothing special," I add, hoping that I'm not hurting my dad's feelings. But my dad's not listen-ing. He's digging out a piece of driftwood with his hands.

"Whoa! Look at this beauty!" my dad says. He holds up a very worn two-by-four board, which is completely barnacle ridden.

Wow.

Without Mommylicious here, my grandma and Dad are taking over her job and making sure that they embarrass me as much as possible.

"What do you guys see when you look at this?" my dad asks.

"I see driftwood," Dylan answers nicely. "Maybe something washed up from the hurricane last year."

"You're probably right," my dad says, and adds the wood to our basket. "But I already have a great vision for what this driftwood can become next. Our house is full of my woodwork."

"That's very cool," Dylan says politely.

I doubt he actually thinks that. Dylan's house is like a modern museum. It's definitely professionally decorated, and there's nothing recycled or old about it.

"You should come by and see some of my pieces sometime," my dad says to Dylan, even though I'm giving my dad the "Are you out of your mind?" stare. "I also have an old surfboard that I'm thinking of repurposing."

"I'd like that," Dylan says, but he's looking at me—not my dad.

"Yes," Grandma Hope chimes in. "I make a great BBQ. I haven't grilled in ages, but now I have some extra time on my hands since I've got this bum wrist. You might not think a lady like me loves to grill, but I sure do. It's important to do anything a man can do and do it better."

Oh em gee, is this happening? Are my grandma and my dad inviting my crush on a family date? Thank God, Mommylicious is not here too; she'd be in overdrive with this content. I can only imagine the blog's headline. "A Boy Finally Talks to Babylicious and the Whole Family Is There to Witness."

Dylan might not find my mom's blog so charming if he ended up featured on it as much as I am. If that happened, he might not think I'm too hard on her.

At the very least, there won't be any pictures to remember this awkward encounter by—although I wouldn't mind a poster of Dylan in his board shorts.

Dylan picks up his paddleboard and puts it under his arm. His biceps ripple with the board's weight. Forget football players—paddleboarders are my type of athlete.

"Well, I'll let you guys go. Have fun with the search," Dylan says.

"See you Monday," I say to Dylan, and sigh with relief as we walk away.

"Don't turn around now, but he's watching you," Grandma Hope whispers into my ear. "I haven't felt that type of eye-heat in a very long time. And what a nice boy! You have great taste."

"Grandma Hope!" I say. "I don't like him. And if I did, I'd be totally mortified by that scene. You and Dad were both, like, flirting with him."

And I am mortified, but maybe my grandma's right. Maybe Dylan is staring at me. Maybe he didn't think it was super-lame that my grandma, my dad, and I hang out. Maybe he will come over for BBQ and to see my dad's old surfboard. Maybe things are changing.

Without Mommylicious here, I feel free, even though I'm technically still grounded. Maybe if we all put down our computers more often and spent that time at the beach, we'd *all* feel freer.

Mommylicious

"BFAB"

Dear Mommylicionados,

First of all, thank you SO much to everyone who came to the Orlando Mom-to-Mom event. I had the BEST time with y'all, and I'm just so flattered that you invited me as your guest speaker. It's hard to believe that most of us had never even met in person before this weekend. But it's like I always say: BFAB! Blog Friends Are Best!

Internet connections are powerful—especially high-speed bandwidth ones. (I know, I know, but I love a good blog joke! Who doesn't?)

Of course, it's always nice to be home, too! I'm very proud of Babylicious for spending some quality time with her dad and grandma. It's totally thrilling (and a bit surprising) that the three of them can survive without me. I think—dare I say it—that they might've even had fun without Mommylicious. It's now hard to believe that once upon a time, Imogene was a total mama's girl.

And three cheers for the fact that Imogene's finally growing out of her rebellious phase just as my awesome readers said she would. It's so nice that y'all can share advice with me just like I've shared it with the Mommylicionados these last sixteen years. After all, that's what blogs are about: sharing what we know and caring for one another.

Now that it's getting closer, I'm starting an official Countdown to BlogHer! Can't wait to see all my fellow bloggers and readers. We're going to rock the Mini-Apple-is! (Hey, that reminds me, cold-weather readers, can I borrow some gloves? Maybe a hat, too?)

Butterfly Kisses,

Mommylicious

PS Still no Pirate's Booty Ball date for Imogene, or at least one that I know of. . . . Hopefully, the girls get smart and get a stag group together! They can go as a gang of wenches. It's always the most fun to hang out with your girls. Isn't that right, my Mommylicionados?

The Mommy Bloggers' Daughters:
The Girl on That Blog

"Unplugged"

I spent the entire weekend grounded and unplugged. I'm turning my computer on for the first time in forty-eight hours—and I'm only back online just to write this blog post.

I was grounded by my mom.

But I unplugged by choice.

We treasure hunted. We ate ice cream. My grandma even grilled.

Nobody clicked. Nobody Tweeted. Nobody Facebooked. Nobody blogged.

There were no check-ins or posed shots to show everyone how much fun we were having.

For the first time in a long time, I felt relaxed. I suggest that everyone try it sometime.

Skulls and Bones,

Babylicious Fights Back

The Mommy Bloggers' Daughters: Life with VeggieMom

"Emeril, Please Adopt Me!"

I spent the day watching the Food Network.

A perfect use of my time since I'm still grounded.

I now wish that Rachael Ray was my mom and Emeril was my dad.

If food is love . . . then why didn't you let me have cotton candy at the spring training game? Mickey pancakes at Disney World? Or cake at anyone's birthday party?

What is life without dessert? Not the type of life that I want to lead.

If we are what we eat, I want to choose what I eat—and therefore, who I am.

VeggieBaby Fights Back

Chapter Ten

THE SAGE WARS

ON MONDAY MORNING I'M EAGERLY WAITING OUTSIDE OF
school at our regular bench for Sage. The second after Ms.
Carter drops her off, I bound toward her.

"Sage!" I exclaim. "I have so much to tell you! I
would've called you, but I committed to going unplugged
for the weekend. And ohmigosh, you won't believe what
happened at the beach Friday, *and* I have this great idea
about how to finally get through to our moms."

I stop to take a breath. Over the weekend, I had a
total epiphany that convincing our moms to unplug for
just one week might be the real answer to our problem. If
they would just step away from the computer, Twitter, and
Facebook, they might not want to go back—or wouldn't
want to go back in the same way. Somehow I need to show

my mom how much better life can be without all of it. Of course, I'll need Sage's help.

I'm about to reveal my revelation when I notice Sage's face is all twisted up.

"Imogene, I know all about your going unplugged. I read your blog about you going all Swiss Family Robinson last night. Did you even see any of my texts?"

Sage puts her hand on her hip and stares at me.

"I only got them this morning. I just told you that I didn't look at my phone or use the computer all weekend minus one blog post, which I'm guessing you must already know from reading my blog."

Sage pauses, then slides right past me toward the lockers, which are housed outside, under an overhang.

Another perk of Florida living.

I follow her and watch as she jams her entire backpack into a locker and slams the door shut so hard that it bangs back open.

I check Sage's fingers and they're especially ripped apart, which means she's super-stressed. Maybe now is not a good time to discuss my idea.

"What's wrong, Sage?" I ask. "I'm sorry I didn't answer your texts earlier, but I'm here now, so let's talk about it. What happened this weekend? Is it about your mom?"

Sage pulls at the skin around her nail beds. "I had a

terrible weekend. I guess it's different for you, but my mom takes the word *grounded* at its Greek origins, so I was actually grounded. Unlike you, being grounded for me means being stuck home alone without anything to do. I definitely was not on any multigenerational beach-capades."

I take that in for a second. I actually *did* have a nice weekend despite being "grounded." I never took the time to think about how Sage was stuck at home the whole weekend. She was probably home with her very angry mom—while I had a break from mine.

"I was pretty much alone for almost two days," Sage continues. "My mom just left me and went on an eighteen-hour date with some organic orange grove farmer. He had a goatee. I mean, really?"

Sage breathes in and starts again. "And what was up with your last post, Imogene? It was all sunshine and rainbows, let's lived unplugged, I had so much fun with my family . . . la-di-da. That's not what the Mommy Bloggers' Daughters is supposed to be about. Our blogs are about trying to get through to our moms that we don't want them to blog about us anymore. And we're supposed to do that by blogging about *them*, not by blogging some manifesto about going unplugged."

I open my mouth to respond, but Sage holds up the palm of her hand like a STOP sign.

"I'm not finished. This whole thing was *your* idea,

Imogene, and *I* got grounded because of it. We're supposed to be taking on our moms and getting them to understand. Now *you're* already totally flaking out on *me* and changing our idea."

Sage pauses and picks at her fingers again. I go to stop her and she pushes my hand away. "I have a thought. Maybe you actually *do* like being Babylicious and getting attention for it. You're probably scared nobody would notice you without your mom's blog. It's clear now that you don't believe in the Mommy Bloggers' Daughters—and maybe you never did."

I've never seen Sage this worked up before. Not even when her mom couldn't afford Sage's piano lessons. Finally Sage's teacher agreed to give her a month of free lessons, which helped to get them through their rough financial period.

"You know that's not true," I say. I speak slow and soft, hoping that it will calm her down. "I'm very sorry, Sage. I didn't know my post would offend you. I think that the Mommy Bloggers' Daughters is about a lot of things. Mostly, it's about getting our moms to stop blogging about us, but I also think it's about trying to get everyone to understand that we aren't who we are online. I think Ms. Herring might've been right. Maybe we *were* being too mean or combative before. We don't have to turn into cyber bullies just to get our point across."

Over the weekend, I spent a lot of time thinking about how invading someone's privacy online isn't really *that* different from cyber bullying. I don't regret starting the Mommy Bloggers' Daughters, but I do want it to evolve into something different from exactly what our moms do to us.

Writing about my mom online didn't make me feel better, but getting away from everything did.

"Sage, I have a great idea," I say with as much cheer as I can muster, after some of the insults she hurled at me. "A really great idea this time. I promise."

"I'm done with your ideas," Sage says. "I bet that you didn't want to be grounded anymore. You're all about the cause . . . until you're grounded. And your grounded does not look like *my* grounded."

"That's not true," I argue, although it was nice to write a post that I knew wouldn't rock the boat too much. I'm sure my mom's already writing some chipper blog post and thinking that this is all over.

But that's still not why I wrote that post. I wrote it because I believed in it.

Sage pushes her tongue against the gap in her teeth. "Are you currently grounded?" Sage accuses.

I pause. My mom ungrounded me this morning after reading my most recent post. She didn't even annoy me about deleting my old posts. She was nearly glowing after reading it, even though she told me that philosophically she disagreed with it, and that having a part of your life online is just as valid as living entirely offline. I think that my mom was just happy the post didn't mention her.

I understand the feeling. I would love not to be on my mom's blog for a day.

"I can get my mom to talk to your mom," I promise Sage. "I bet your mom will unground you, too."

Sage stomps her foot on the ground. "Imogene, it's *not* about being ungrounded," she says. "It is about my mom listening. It's about *our* moms listening. It's about us accomplishing what we said we would," she says loudly enough that other people look toward us. "We said that this year would be different."

I look at Sage, unsure of what to say. This year has already been different for me.

From over my shoulder, I hear a voice.

"Hi, Sage. Hi, Imogene," Dylan says as he spins his lock about ten feet away.

"Imogene, do you and your family go beachcombing a lot?" he asks. "Your dad seemed pretty stoked about it—like, 'maybe he should get a cable TV show about it' stoked."

Sage looks at me as if I'm a stranger and she turns and walks away. Her locker is still wide open.

I breathe in and shut Sage's locker for her.

"My dad's a big nerd," I say to Dylan, trying to regain my composure as I watch Sage stalk off. "He loves making things from what he finds beachcombing."

"I think that it's cool," Dylan says. "My dad can't even fix a rusty door hinge. Well, not that our door hinges are rusty, but you know what I mean." Dylan grabs another book out of his locker. "By the way, I liked your post about going unplugged. I wish I could convince my family to have a weekend like that, but I'm pretty sure that my parents' fingers are superglued to their BlackBerries. We live a tenth of a mile from the beach, and they haven't touched the sand in months."

I stand there, not knowing what to say. Dylan Mulberry, *the* Dylan, thinks my family is sort of cool *and* he's admitting that he reads my blog.

Reading someone's blog is like online crushing, right?

What alternate universe am I living in?

Oh yeah, one where my best friend is mad at me. But also one where I'm not grounded and where some guy—who I really like—might actually like me back.

Sage doesn't show up to lunch, so I sit with Mackenzie and Anne. I'm hoping that this will all blow over soon, but I'm not so sure. Sage seemed so angry with me, and is definitely not going to be onboard for going unplugged. She seems intent on taking the Mommy Bloggers' Daughters

Version One across the finish line.

During lunch Anne splits her veggie and California rolls with me. Her parents own Sushi-Thai Too, a local Asian fusion restaurant on Fifth Avenue.

"Imogene," Mackenzie says, "your unplugged post was cool. I'm going to show it to my mom. She's, like, ruining my younger sister's life by documenting every second of it. Last summer she posted a video of my sister's recital online for the world to see . . . except my sister is the worst dancer ever. How is that helping her to have that online? She's going to be totally haunted. Hello, Mom, not all kid pictures are cute, and nobody wants to see a million of them."

Anne nods. "That's brutal," she says. "At my cousins' Little League games, none of the parents—minus one crazy, obsessed guy who the refs always end up kicking out—actually watch the game. Everyone is on their phones the *entire* time." Anne leans forward. "Get this: My cousin hit a home run and there was, like, delayed applause. She was on second base before the parents caught on. It was hilarious, but sad, too."

Mackenzie slaps the table. "I know! Then adults go all pyscho on *us* for spending too much time online. Hello, you all do it too. And my parents are making me update their website. Ugh! I'm sick of computers and HTM—whatever you call it."

I shrug. "I could help you," I say. Despite disliking my mom's blog, I've definitely picked up a few things about HTML code over the years. My mom has always told me that it's going to get me places in the work world, but until now, I've ignored her. Even though it pays the bills, I still hate to think of my mom's job as work. Isn't it illegal to make money off your kid? Isn't that why child stars sue their own parents?

As we're gathering up our trash, Ardsley and Tara approach our table. She usually sits with Tara and some other girls, right near Dylan and his guy friends' table.

I think she spends more of lunchtime posing than eating.

"Hi, Mackenzie. Hi, Anne," she says flatly.

I expect Ardsley to ignore me, which is what she usually does if she's not harassing me about my mom's blog.

"Imogene," she coos instead, surprising me. "Can I speed-dial in a favor? I need some help with my blog. And I thought, who better than you—Babylicious?"

"Are you serious?" I ask before I can think twice.

Ardsley nods. "I'm trying hard to keep my grades up this year since they, like, count now, and I definitely want to go to a fashion college in New York City." Ardsley makes jazz hands. "And I happen to have this totally visionary idea for a fashion blog, but I need some help. I could do something for you in return," she says. She looks me up and down as if I need a lot of her help.

Mackenzie and Anne stare at me and wait for my answer. As much as I love Sage, I'm glad that she's not here. She would make this into a total scene and rattle off the top twenty-five reasons why I shouldn't help Ardsley.

This year is about being different, I remind myself.

So I say yes before I can change my mind.

"Perfect, we'll figure it all out in English class. Toodles, ladies," Ardsley says before she swaggers off. Tara follows in her shadow.

I'm hoping it really is a better life philosophy to say, "Why not?" than to ask, "Why?"

"Stop packing up, guys," Ms. Herring admonishes us. "I'm *not* done with you yet. I still have one hundred and twenty seconds of your time and I'm using every one."

Teachers, especially during our last period, hate it when we start putting our books away early, but we always do it anyway.

"Before you all go, I just wanted to say that I've been very impressed with some of your blogs lately. A lot of you are taking the big step from private to public. But even more than that, I'm ecstatic that some of you are writing about your interests and beliefs." Ms. Herring puts her hand on her heart. "I think when you blog about something you love, something special happens on the internet.

I know that sounds hokey, but I think positive things can happen from sharing your passions online. That's all. You can go now."

Sage rolls her eyes. "She's wrong. Nothing special happens," she says in a soft voice.

I lean in close, happy that Sage's actually talking to me. She continues, "People write about their interests on the internet, so that random strangers will stop by and give them an ego boost. Blogging is the same as fishing for compliments. It's all about trying to find strangers to pump you up since no one in your real life cares."

"But what about the people who disagree with you? Both our moms definitely have their share of haters," I say.

My mom has even had to block some people's IP addresses after they've left mean or creepy comments.

"Just because people don't like what you blog about doesn't mean that they're haters, Imogene. They're just trying to start a dialogue, but most of the time bloggers just ignore them and call them trolls. Our moms are treating us like trolls right now. They don't care what we think, even if we are right. We're their daughters and they should have to listen to us."

Trolls are people who write mean things on the internet. In my mom's office, there's a giant poster with a photo of a Troll droll with an *X* through it.

Sage doesn't make a move to leave, so I try to get up

the courage to bring up this morning.

"I'm sorry about earlier," I say. "It sucks that you had a tough weekend. I didn't mean to hurt your feelings with my post at all. I'm still for trying to get our moms to stop blogging about us. I really do hate being Babylicious. I just want to figure out the best way to stop them."

Sage turns to make sure the classroom is empty. "How come you didn't tell me about seeing Dylan at the beach?"

"I just told you. I wanted a weekend away from technology, and I was grounded, so I couldn't go tell you in person," I say. I'm trying not to get frustrated with Sage. "I said I was sorry."

Sage gets up and grabs her bag. "Did you want a weekend away from technology or a weekend away from me?"

I stand up just as quickly. "What are you talking about?" I ask. "You're my best friend. You've always been my best friend."

Sage is losing it, I think.

Just then, Ardsley peers into the classroom.

"Oh, good! You're still here, Imogene. I almost forgot about our blog date. Let's do tomorrow at six at my house," Ardsley says. "Toodles."

Sage throws up her hands. "Excuse me?" she says after Ardsley bops off.

"I know," I say, and shake my head. "Who says 'toodles'?"

Sage picks up her foot as if she's going to stomp again. Her foots hovers in midair for a moment before she gently sets it down. She points at me. "You know that's not what I meant, Imogene. I want to know why you are going to Ardsley's house," she says. She barges through the classroom toward the door.

"I told her that I'd help her with her blog," I admit, and I can almost feel the sparks flying from Sage's green eyes. She's actually named for the color, not the seasoning. Her mom has the same eyes. They both breathe green fire when they're mad.

I wait for Sage's wrath, but she doesn't say anything.

I feel relieved, even though I know that this is far from over.

Just as we reach the doorway, Sage turns to me and lowers her voice.

"Ardsley's blog is called 'Mermaids, Manicures, and Macaroons.' Does that even make sense? I thought we're trying to get people to realize that blogs, especially our moms' blogs, are annoying and pointless. But all of a sudden, you're now *helping* Ardsley with her stupid blog while also going around preaching for people to get offline? Hypocrite, lately? I feel like I don't even know you."

I don't even know how to defend myself. Sage has gone totally militant. It's like I can't do anything right.

"What's this all about?" I ask her. "Why are you *so* mad at me?"

Sage bites her lip. "I'm mad because you were so not actually grounded this weekend like me. I'm mad because you didn't tell me about Dylan or about Ardsley. I'm mad because you're too wrapped up in the fact your blog is getting you attention, and you don't care about the real purpose of our blogs anymore. You're probably too blind to see it, but you're just like your mom now."

I take a step back into the hallway. "That's not fair," I say. "Yes, my mom's totally annoying, but it's not your place to insult her. Maybe if you spent less time playing the piano and less time being all agro, you'd have more friends too, Sage. Have you ever thought that I'm making friends because people like me, not because of some blog?"

I pivot in the hallway and walk away from Sage. I'm unsure—for the first time ever—if we are still best friends.

Chapter Eleven

I'VE ALREADY SAID YES

SAGE'S WORDS *YOU'RE JUST LIKE YOUR MOM* REPEAT IN MY HEAD over and over during swim practice. No matter how much I speed up or how many flip turns I do, I can still hear them. Nothing—not even two hours of swimming—can drown them out.

Sage *knows* that I'm nothing like my mom, so why would she say that? Every single person in our class has a blog, so it's ridiculous that she thinks I'm using mine as leverage for anything, especially popularity. Yes, my blog has gotten attention, but so has Sage's. Why is she suddenly treating me like the enemy? And why did it hurt so badly when she insulted my mom?

As I shake the water out of my ears after practice, I decide two things: 1) I'm definitely not like my mom, and 2) Sage is acting ridiculous.

When I get home, my grandma notices right away that I'm out of sorts.

"I know what puppy love looks like, and that's not your face. What's going on, Georgia?" she asks as I help her carry kabobs from the grill. Earlier, Grandma Hope told me that she'd decided to stop feeling sorry for herself and start doing some more one-armed cooking.

"I'm fine. I'm fine," I insist.

"Meg!" Grandma Hope calls out toward my mom's office. "Dinner!"

"I'm working on something for the blog," my mom calls out.

"Even God took a day to rest," my grandma calls back.

"God didn't have a blog," my mom says. "I'll be there in one minute!"

"I'm not smelling like charcoal instead of my Charlemagne perfume for you to make us wait!" my grandma yells.

My dad looks up from the table where he's going over some blueprints, and grins. "You tell her!" he teases with a wink.

"I just think that we need to put some more family back into this place. A house is just a house, but a home is where family is. We need to work to make this place a home," Grandma Hope says with a scoff. "I had such a nice weekend, and I figure we might as well enjoy one another before I go back to my birdies and eagles."

Birdies and *eagles* are more Golf-speak.

"I had a great time too," my dad says, standing up and going over to the sink to wash his hands. "Thanks for distracting me from all this." He nods back toward his blueprints.

Like always, my dad has a bit of ink on his hands and his clothes. Even though most architects now work only on computers, my dad always starts his designs the old-fashioned way, by hand. He's retro like that. He and my mom are classic examples of opposites attracting.

Grandma Hope steps into the hallway. "Meg! Now!" she shouts.

My mom sheepishly emerges from her office and sits down at the table.

She looks down at a coffee stain on her blouse. "I feel fourteen," my mom says. "My mom's cooking for me. My mom's bossing me around. It's like I'm still a little kid."

"I can get that stain out for you. And, Meg, you'll always be my child," Grandma Hope says. "Speaking of children, something's wrong with *yours*. Georgia's got this sad look on her face. For Pete's sake, it's even worse than Rory McIlroy's face when he four-putted in the Masters. No matter what he does from here on out, that's how he's going to be remembered."

I pull a shrimp off my kabob. "Grandma Hope!" I say. "I'm completely fine." I add a smile for effect. I grind my teeth.

My dad puts his blueprints back into his briefcase and snaps it shut.

"Is Hope right, Imogene? Is something wrong?"

I shake my head and grind through another smile.

My mom reaches over me for an ear of grilled corn. "Imogene seems A-OK to me."

Despite the fact that my mom has blogged about me every single day of my life, she still doesn't really know me as well as Grandma Hope does. She can't even tell that I'm sad right now. Like, I'm probably as upset as I was when my grandpa died. Maybe my mom's so used to my fake smile that she can't even differentiate it from my real smile. That makes me even sadder.

"I have big news everyone," my mom says, changing the subject. "I didn't want to say anything in case it fell through, but Imogene and I were selected for a panel at BlogHer! Isn't that great? We'll be speaking about moms and daughters who blog. Super-great, huh? The panels are a *major* big deal, so this is going to be dynamite for reader-ship, not to mention sponsors. Maybe it'll help you funnel some traffic to your site, Imogene, but of course, you'll need to get rid of some of your early posts first."

Wait. My mom—who threatened to ground me over

my blog—is now using it for publicity for *her* blog?

Actually, this is so *not* shocking.

I focus on my kabob. "I don't want to do the panel," I say. "You know that I hate public speaking," I add, which is true.

"It's in less than three weeks," my mom says, "and I already told them yes—"

"Hold on," my dad interrupts from the sink, where he's washing his hands.

"End of the conversation. Period," my mom says, dismissing my dad with a wave.

Grandma Hope raises her eyebrows, and my dad looks down at his plate.

I start to argue more, but then I have a flash of genius. If my mom is going to make me do this panel, I'll make sure she regrets it. And I've just thought of the perfect plan to make sure that happens.

We eat the rest of our meal silently, aside from the constant chime of my mom's phone.

After everyone's finished, my mom stands up, takes a few steps, and holds her phone away at arm's length.

Click goes the phone, but my mom's the only one who's smiling.

After I wash the dishes, I go to my room. I briefly think about calling Sage before I remember that we're fighting.

Suddenly I feel very alone.

★ ★ ★

The next morning, Sage isn't waiting for me outside of school at our bench. She doesn't show up to lunch, either, so I sit with Mackenzie and Anne again.

"Imogene, are you in a fight with Sage?" Anne asks. "Andrew's words, not mine. I should've guessed, since you two are normally, like, conjoined at the hip."

"We're not in a fight exactly," I say. I don't really want to get into it with Anne and Mackenzie. "Sage's probably just practicing piano in the band room. She's very serious about her future. She's trying to get into Juilliard."

Anne pours soy sauce from a small container and shakes her head.

"Andrew said it has something to do with your blogs."

When did Andrew become such a gossip? And why is Sage telling him about our fight?

Mackenzie grabs a piece of a California roll from Anne's plate. "If you guys *are* in a fight, I bet that you didn't hear that Sage got asked to the Pirate's Booty Ball. I think she's the first girl in our class to be asked."

I drop my tuna-fish sandwich on my tray.

"What?"

"Yup. Andrew asked her last night, but she didn't say yes, exactly, because she's not sure if she'll still be grounded by then."

"Oh. Good for her," I say, but I can't force myself to

smile. "She and Andrew have a lot in common."

I'm trying to make it sound like I don't care. But I do care. It's Sage and I who have a lot in common. Or at least, we used to.

And it's bad enough that Sage and I are in a fight, but it's even worse that something actually important happened to her and I wasn't the one she told. Getting asked to our first real dance is a huge deal, and we always go to each other first when something big happens.

"Andrew, like, practically begged me to ask you to get Sage to quit this whole blog thing, so she can go to the dance. He's got it bad for her," Mackenzie says. She frowns. "I wish a guy liked me like that."

"Sage's blog is up to Sage," I say. "Please tell Andrew I don't have any control over that."

Which is true. Sage made it perfectly clear that she didn't want anything to do with me right now.

The thought of talking about this anymore or eating the rest of my sandwich makes me feel queasy, so I get up, mutter an excuse, and spend the rest of lunch in the girls' locker room, trying not to cry.

When I walk into English class, Sage's already there. But she's not sitting in her usual seat up front. She's sitting in the back row, which is something Sage's never done before.

She's just not a back-row kid.

I walk right past her without a word.

If anyone's apologizing, it should be her. I still can't stop the words *You're just like your mom* from swimming in my head.

Because Sage has upset the seating balance, Dylan—who always sits in the back row and *is* a back-row kid—is forced to sit next to me in Sage's empty seat when he shows up late.

A few days ago, sitting next to Dylan would've made my week, but right now I'm just too depressed to care.

After class, Ardsley sashays her way up to my desk.

"You're on the swim team, right?" Ardsley asks.

I nod.

"I thought so. You have this green tinge to your hair. It totally gives swimmers away. Any-who, I'll have my mom pick you up after your practice and bring you over to help me with my blog."

Ardsley scampers off, and Dylan, who's still packing up his backpack, starts laughing.

"Is she for real?"

I force a laugh, but in reality, I just want to get to a mirror to see if my hair actually is turning green.

"It's not green," Dylan says as if he's reading my mind. "It's brown, but a pretty brown, if that makes sense."

"Thanks," I say, but Dylan's already heading out the door.

If Sage and I weren't in a fight, we'd totally have a major squeal over that moment.

Instead I walk to the pool alone.

During swim practice, I try to think of excuses to get out of helping Ardsley.

My grandma's hurt and needs my help.

Sort of true, but my grandma doesn't need my help. She's probably grilling half a cow right now.

I need to see a hairdresser about my green hair.

Hopefully not true.

My former best friend and I are in a huge fight. She thinks that I flaked out on our mission, and I think that she's being crazy. And I also can't stop thinking about how she said I was just like my mom.

Definitely all true, but I don't want to tell Ardsley any of that.

But if I go home, there will be just more questions from Grandma Hope about my sad face and more nagging from my mom about preparing for BlogHer. I decide to suck it up and go to Ardsley's house. At least my mom can't take pictures of me or mention BlogHer when I'm not home.

As promised, Ardsley's mother is waiting for me in our school's parking lot.

"Imogene, over here!" she calls out of her car's window.

I get in and focus on deep breathing. Don't think about BlogHer. Don't think about Sage. Just get through tonight.

Mrs. Taylor starts the car and we head toward Ardsley's house—somewhere I probably haven't visited since Ardsley's seventh birthday party.

Despite my feelings toward Ardsley, I've always really liked Mrs. Taylor. Every year, when the PE teachers force us to run the mile (which is inhumane—especially in the Florida heat), she always brings everyone juice boxes and granola bars to eat after we finish.

"Imogene, I just wanted to thank you for helping Ardsley with her blog," Mrs. Taylor says.

"No problem," I say. "I have a *little* experience with blogs," I joke.

Mrs. Taylor smiles. "No, *really*, it's very kind. School's never been Ardsley's brightest spot, but she's been really excited about her blog. I'm hoping that this might be something that helps build her self-confidence."

Ardsley needs help building her self-confidence? I find *that* hard to believe.

This conversation reminds of me what Sage said about how blogs are really just ways for people to feel good about themselves, and I wonder if she's right. But I also wonder if that's a truly terrible thing.

Did I use my blog to gain friends and self-confidence? Am I like my mom and Ardsley?

I shake the thoughts from my head. After all, I'm the one who thought of the Mommy Bloggers' Daughters and I didn't start it to become popular. I started it to show my mom something. Just because Sage doesn't like the way I'm doing it now, doesn't mean that I'm wrong.

"So thank you, Imogene," Mrs. Taylor repeats as we pull into the driveway. "This is going to really help Ardsley since I know that you're very well versed in blogs."

Too well versed, I silently add. It's practically my first language—one I'm always wishing I could forget.

I find Ardsley sprawled out on her bedroom's pink carpet. Scattered all around her are fashion magazine and newspaper article cutouts. In a corner of her room, there's a hanging rack overflowing with colorful clothes. The metal rod is literally bending from the clothes' weight.

Ardsley catches me staring at it as I take in the room. She shrugs. "Not all my clothes can fit in my closet," she admits. "Clothes are my thing with a capital *T*, so it's barbaric that we attend a school with uniforms. I can't wait for the tenth grade, when I'm finally liberated from polyester. It's going to feel like I was released from prison."

I raise my eyebrows at her analogy and find a spot on the floor among the clippings.

"Thanks for coming," Ardsley adds. She turns her laptop to face me.

"Sure," I say. "What do you want help with?"

"I've read all these articles about teens who've become famous fashion bloggers. One girl—she's not even from New York City—gets a front-row seat at fashion week. I want to become her. Or at least become just like her. Can you help me?" Ardsley nearly glows with excitement.

She looks like my mom when she talks about her blog.

I hesitate, thinking about how I don't actually believe in blogging. How I think blogging is a waste of time and how much I wish that my mom would stop doing it. Then I think about how blogging's what came between Sage and me. Finally I think about how I have an entire plan, with a capital *P*, as Ardsley would say, to stop my mom at BlogHer.

But I also see how sincerely interested Ardsley is, and how she's treating me (almost) nicely for the first time in my life. I also remember what her mom said in the car.

I hand Ardsley a pen and a paper from my bag.

"Okay, Ardsley, you need to start taking notes because I'm about to give you a crash course in blogging one-oh-one. Let's start with your brand. What makes you special? What's your fashion blog going to offer readers that no other blog can? What's the best design to attract *and* keep readers?"

Three hours later, I stumble out of Ardsley's house. I'm exhausted and I'm surprised on two levels. First, Ardsley's actually not that bad one-on-one, and second, I'm pretty good at this blogging thing.

It's too bad that I hate it so much.

Mommylicious

"Great News, Great News, Read All about It."

Dear Mommylicious Readers,

As you might've guessed, I have some great—okay, fantastic—news.

Imogene and I are honored to announce that we've been selected for a panel at BlogHer. We'll be talking about what it's like to be a mother-and-daughter blogging duo. (And I promise, I'll pass on Imogene's blog URL once it's up and ready for consumption! She's still working on some nuts and bolts. . . .)

I'm so excited for the conference, and I just can't wait to share my thoughts with all of you! I love BlogHer because I can finally give my readers real hugs rather than virtual ones. ☺

Plus, I can't wait to spend some QT with Imogene. Why doesn't anyone tell you that part of your kids growing up means that they grow apart from you?

In other news, Imogene has her first swim meet of the year soon, and I promise to live Tweet you the results. She's not Olympic material . . . yet, but I'm still one proud swim momma.

What about y'all? Are you the ones in the stands hollering and cheering? Or are you the silent but supportive types?

How do we encourage our kids but not overwhelm them?

Butterfly Kisses,

Mommylicious

PS Rumors are flying that boys are starting to ask girls to the Pirate's Booty Ball. Cross your fingers that someone's smart enough to snag Imogene! Where'd my baby go? Or should I say where'd *our* baby go?

The Mommy Bloggers' Daughters: The Girl on That Blog

"Why Do We Blog?"

Lately I've been up late, wondering why humans blog.

Or rather, why do *some* humans blog?

One day will everyone document their lives for people they don't know? Will it be a basic need like food or water?

Is it about gaining confidence?

Finding friends?

Is it about sharing expertise? Or sharing experiences?

Is it about being heard?

I'm wondering if I've been against blogging for so long that I've forgotten to see the other sides.

But still,

Don't Dare Call Me Babylicious

The Mommy Blogger's Daughter: Life with VeggieMom

"On Not Giving Up on What You Believe In"

Every celebrity says that they hate fame. It's so awful, they cry.

They act all surprised, as if they didn't know it was part of the career description.

"Ohmigosh," a celebrity squeals, "I didn't become famous to get free stuff, be on magazine covers, and have everyone want to be me."

"It's so miserable," they repeat over and over.

I say it's all BS.

If you believe in privacy, you have to fight for it.

Sometimes, you even have to sacrifice what you love most for your privacy.

I'm becoming a freedom fighter and starting today, I'm quitting the piano and going on a piano strike in protest of my mom's blog. In protest against all the invasive mommy bloggers out there.

And, Andrew, I'm sorry, but I'm definitely still grounded, so I can't go to the dance.

VeggieBaby Fights Back

PS I'm on day three of an all-you-can-eat junk-food "cleanse" and I've never felt better. Message me for the "diet." It's awesome. It involves eating all the colors you can't find in nature. Bright orange makes up the base of the pyramid. Hello, Doritos (snack strong!) and Cheetos (it ain't easy being cheesy)!

Chapter Twelve

THE ALLIGATORS AREN'T THE ONLY THINGS THAT BITE

I'M TRYING TO FIND MY SCRUBBIEST PAIR OF SWEATPANTS IN THE back of my closet, the part that's dark and holds remnants from years past. While I'm on my hands and knees, digging through Halloween costumes from elementary school, I hear someone clear her throat.

I whip around to see my mom standing above me.

I quickly check to see that she doesn't have a camera anywhere on her, especially since I'm wearing only a silk robe, another gift from one of my mom's sponsors.

"What do you want, Mom? I'm trying to find a pair of sweatpants for our swamp walk. Mr. Swenson told us three times that whatever we wear is going to get destroyed. We're going through, like, three biospheres or atmospheres or something—I can't remember what they're called."

My mom gets down on her hands and knees. She pulls out the bottom drawer of my dresser and reaches into the very back of it.

My mom tugs out a pair of gray sweats with LITTLE DOLPHIN, sewn in patch letters, written across the butt. "Are these what you're looking for?"

I take the pants from her. "Thanks," I say. "I think it's finally time to say hey, hey, good-bye to these."

I wait for my mom to leave so I can finish getting ready.

She doesn't take the cue. Instead she repositions herself and sits cross-legged on my floor.

"Can we talk, Imogene?"

"My last two posts weren't even about you, Mom," I say. "I think I'm done with that whole idea of trying to get you to change by posting about you. It obviously didn't work. And by the way, please stop writing about the Pirate's Booty Ball. I don't need the whole world to know that I don't have a date. It's bad enough that the whole school knows it."

My mom stands up, extends her hand to me, and pulls me up off the ground. "This isn't about your blog. Or my blog, for that matter."

"Is it about BlogHer? We still have over two weeks to work on the panel," I say. "And besides, I don't even want to do it."

I don't mention that I have the Plan for when she *does* make me do it.

"It's not about BlogHer, either," my mom says. "But you're doing the panel, no ifs, ands, or buts. We've made a commitment, and we're keeping it. The Mommylicious name means something, and I intend for it to stay that way."

It's funny that my mom cares more about what strangers think of her than her own daughter. Good thing my mom can't read my mind; she'd flip if she knew about the Plan. What will strangers think after I follow through on that?

I roll my eyes and start tossing fresh clothes into a bag to put on after the swamp walk.

"Well, can you just blog about whatever you want to talk to me about? Because I'm sort of in a hurry here?"

My mom laughs. "You're getting funny in your old age," she teases. "But this is serious, Imogene. I want to talk to you about Sage."

I stop and ball a pair of socks into a tight fist in my hand. Slowly, I turn around.

I look down at the carpet. "What about her?"

It's been nearly a week since Sage and I last spoke. I knew that eventually Sage's mom would talk to my mom, but I've been holding my breath and hoping it would all be resolved before it came to this. I've also been holding out that Sage would apologize. Plus, I want to tell her about the Plan!

My mom bends down and picks out an old pair of Keds from a pile of shoes. "Wear these, honey. Keds are never coming back in style. I'm not sure why they were ever in style, come to think of it. Anyway, Zoey—I mean Ms. Carter—is really worried about Sage. She thinks that Sage is going through a bit of a life squall. She's threatening not to go to BlogHer, and Ms. Carter said Sage's post from last night was about how she has quit the piano."

"Sage is quitting piano?" I feel as if I've been knocked down by a wave and don't know which way is up anymore.

"Didn't you read her latest blog post?" my mom asks. Her face looks like I've committed a cardinal sin.

The truth is I've been afraid to read Sage's blog lately because I'm afraid she'll write about me—and our fight.

"Why would she ever quit?" I ask. "That's plain *stupid*."

My mom shrugs. "I don't know. I guess she's doing it as a protest against blogging. I'm not sure how that even makes sense, but that's what Ms. Carter told me on the phone."

"But Sage *loves* the piano," I say. "And she doesn't *just* love the piano. It's her dream. It's what she does."

Ever since I've known her, Sage has always played the piano. It's an extension of who she is.

"Ms. Carter is under the impression that you two might be in a fight, but she's still hoping that you can try to talk some sense into Sage since you're her best friend."

I shake my head. "I'm not so sure that she'll listen," I say.

My mom hands me the sunscreen from my dresser. "Put this on," she instructs. "It's going to be hot in the swamp. And please, Imogene, *try* talking to her. It's not easy for Ms. Carter having to deal with Sage all on her own."

I want to tell my mom that it's not easy for Sage to deal with Ms. Carter on her own either, but instead I say, "I'll make you a deal. If you don't post anything else on your blog about the Pirate's Booty Ball, I promise you that I'll talk to Sage."

"Are you bargaining with me right now?" my mom asks, her eyes wide. "This is about your best friend and her welfare, honey."

I zip my bag up. "Deal or no deal?"

If I'm going to be brave enough to talk to Sage, I better get something out of it.

My mom sighs. "Deal, but I still get the photo rights to the actual dance."

"Fine," I concede.

I gag a little bit over what's just transpired. Photo rights? Who *is* she? TMZ? *Us Weekly*?

I don't mention that I probably won't even go to the dance anyway, since I'm both friendless and dateless. My mom can have the photo rights to me moping on the couch.

I try to slip past my mom, but she demands a hug. She wouldn't want one if she only knew what I was planning for BlogHer. I move away from her grasp and quickly head down the stairs.

From behind me, I can hear my mom scampering toward her bedroom. "Imogene, you are not permitted to leave before I get a photo. You will look so cute in your swamp clothes!" she calls. "Most of my readers don't live in Florida. They're going to eat this swamp thing right up."

Quickly, I race out the door and to the bus stop. While I might have made a barter with my mom to talk to Sage, I'm still not consenting to have my picture taken in sweatpants I wore four years ago.

When you attend a school with uniforms, any day that you don't have to wear a uniform feels like a party, even if you're all just wearing swamp clothes to go investigate the Everglades for biology class.

The entire ninth grade has congregated in the cafeteria, where the teachers are taking attendance. Everyone's talking loudly, and you can see bits of everyone's personality popping out from his or her clothes. For once, we look like individuals rather than a mob of polyester-wearing teenagers.

I spot Sage and Andrew sitting on top of a lunch table in the corner.

I guess now is not the best time to make good on my promise to talk to Sage.

Despite giving up the piano and being in a fight with her best friend, Sage looks pretty happy and is laughing loudly at everything Andrew says. She's also tossing her curls at a rate of five times for every ten seconds. That's a lot of curl tossing.

Then it dawns on me that I have no one to sit with on the bus. I've sat with Sage for all our field trips, like the one to SeaWorld in third grade. I try to tell myself that it's ninth grade and I shouldn't care who I sit with on the bus, but I'm lying to myself—because I do care.

"Imogene Luden?" Ms. Swenson calls out.

"Here," I reply. "I'm here," I repeat. I feel lost even though I'm in the same cafeteria I've eaten in daily for the past ten years.

I feel a tap on my shoulder and turn around to find Dylan.

"No need to be nervous," he says. "The chance of being attacked by an alligator is only one in twenty-four million. It's true we have the worst odds living in Florida, but you are still more likely to be struck by lightning."

I see Sage peering over at us, so I put on my best fake smile, the one where you can see nearly all my teeth, and turn to Dylan.

"The zigzag thing is a lie, by the way. If an alligator is chasing you, you should run straight. You're more likely to fall if you run in a zigzag pattern. If you run straight ahead, the alligator will probably tire out before you do. They're not very good long-distance runners."

"I guess you Googled all this too," Dylan says with a laugh.

I laugh too, because I'm very happy to have company, especially Dylan's company.

"The internet's got to be good for something, even if it's only keeping us safe from alligators."

"I read your last post," Dylan says. "I liked it. I like your blog. Mine is so lame. Anyway, I'll see you later—alligator."

"Very funny. Bye, Dylan," I say. I use two fingers and point at his face. "Remember to go for the eyes if you get attacked."

I end up sitting alone on the bus. It isn't the worse thing ever.

But it's pretty bad.

I pick out a seat in the very front and eavesdrop on the teachers' debate over the quality of the coffee selection in the teachers' lounge.

Sage and Andrew walk right past me when they board. I hope Sage finally realizes that my blog definitely hasn't made me popular.

I'm down a friend because of it.

As our bus makes its way down Interstate 75, I think about how much has happened in the last few months. I could've never guessed any of this back on the first day of school. I had hoped for change, but I guess change doesn't always create the picture you designed in your head.

Finally, after driving on a desolate highway and passing a few Seminole reservations, we arrive at the Clyde Butcher Gallery. Clyde Butcher is a famous local photographer, well known for his black-and-white photographs of the Everglades. (He also looks like a lot like Santa Claus.) We studied him in art class, and I think he's a total badass. In order to get his famous shots, he becomes part of the swamp, often wading out in the pitch-black of night and waiting for the first light.

His gallery and home are here, right in the middle of the Everglades. October through March, when alligators aren't nesting, you can take a swamp walk of the property. It's perfect for the ninth grade because we just finished a unit on the Everglades.

When we get off the bus, someone immediately spots a baby alligator swimming around in the water under a small bridge. If you're from Florida and you're over the age of eight, you've probably seen an alligator before, but it's still exciting each time.

After that enthusiasm dies down, the teachers round us up. Ms. Herring announces that she'll stay at the gallery and watch an educational DVD with anyone who feels uncomfortable with the swamp walk, which makes me wish there had been an option like that for the blog project.

If we had just opted out, Sage and I wouldn't be in this fight.

And she'd still be playing the piano.

But I would've never told my mom how I felt. Yes, even though she's still blogging about me, I'm glad that I've finally started to tell her how I feel. Even if it hasn't really made a difference to her yet, it's made a difference to me.

Also, without the blog project, Dylan would've never talked to me about my blog either.

I guess I'll admit that the blog thing hasn't been all terrible. It's funny how you want to separate events in your life into either good or bad piles, but sometimes, the same thing fits into both categories.

Mr. Swenson lists off the names in each group. Of course, I'm in the same small group with Ardsley, Sage, and Dylan. The teachers probably thought they were being nice by putting me with Sage. Little do they know . . .

Our leader is Mr. Johnson, our algebra teacher. Every

day, he carries a protractor in his pocket, and today's no exception—despite the fact we're dredging through a swamp. Unless the ability to measure a right angle is going to save us from the alligators, Mr. Johnson's not going to be much help in an emergency.

We walk closer to the swamp's perimeter to meet our tour guide.

Dylan points at me. "Remember your promise," he says. "You're going to save me if I get attacked."

Sage rolls her eyes at me and makes a gagging motion.

I guess that means we're definitely still in a fight.

"Hello!" a young woman, probably in her twenties, dressed in head-to-toe khaki says, greeting our group. "Welcome to the Everglades! I'm Raine, and I'll be your leader for the day. We're going on a swamp walk, which is also called a muck-about. I've been a national park guide for several years, so please trust that I know what I'm doing." Raine digs her walking stick into the mud. "We'll be wading through water that can reach as high as your waist, so it can be hard to see what's going on down there. I'm going to pass out walking sticks to everyone, and you're going to use those to feel out any roots that might be in your way. If you're leading the group, and everyone will get a chance to lead, you'll need to make sure you call out 'root' to the group so that no one trips over one." Raine looks around and gives a smile that only a tour guide could muster. "I can already tell this is going to be an awesome time!"

Mr. Johnson nods, but he doesn't look so certain. I think he'd rather be teaching the quadratic formula for the fortieth year than going into this swamp.

"Are we going to see an adult alligator?" Ardsley asks.

Raine shakes her head. "Doubtful," she replies. "We take great care to avoid them and their areas. We also have a tacit agreement with their king to keep to our side of the swamp. Just kidding!"

We don't laugh.

"But truthfully, we do try to avoid them. In my four years of doing this, I've seen only one alligator while on a swamp walk, and it was a teeny tiny one—probably only six feet."

"Six feet is *teeny tiny*?" Ardsley has turned alligator green. "Can I go back? I'm not sure this is for me."

"Go right ahead," Mr. Johnson says, pointing toward the way we came. "It's your choice."

Quickly, Ardsley hightails it back to the gallery. Mr. Johnson looks like he wants to follow her.

Now my small group consists of Raine, Sage, Dylan, Mr. Johnson, and me. Awkward.com.

"Who wants to lead?"

Sage raises my hand for me. "Imogene does," she says. "She's a leader and she just loves coming up with great ideas."

I pull my arm down. Now it's my turn to roll my eyes at Sage.

Dylan takes a step forward. "I'll lead," he says. "I want to be the first one to see an alligator."

Raine shakes her head and frowns. "Hey, guys, we'll be seeing lots of cool birds and plants, but no alligators. There's so much more to the Everglades than alligators, and by the end of this walk, you'll think so too. Tour Guide Promise."

As we approach the edge of the swamp, Dylan, along with his wooden walking stick, takes the lead. I follow Mr. Johnson and Raine, and Sage takes up the rear.

"Halt!" Raine calls out to the group. "Over here!"

All of us gather around Raine, who asks us if we see anything. She's pointing at a bare bush, so all of us shake our heads.

"Keep looking," she says to encourage us.

Sage points at a minuscule yellow blossom on a branch. "Is *that* it?"

"Yes!" Raine exclaims. "That's a jingle bell orchid. The smallest orchid in Florida. Usually, I stump students with that. You must have a good eye for detail."

I want to tell Sage that the orchid reminds me of her because it's so tiny, but then I remember—we're not speaking.

We continue on, and the landscape changes from barren to very lush with tons of green ferns and orange-and-red plants everywhere.

Raine makes a sweeping gesture with her free hand. "We're entering a new biosphere now. Do you see how everything has changed in an instant? The trees are different. The colors are different. The temperature has even dropped."

I look back, and I can see the line that divides this new biosphere from the old one. I see Sage staring at me and think how my life feels like two biospheres, the one before the Mommy Bloggers' Daughters and the one after. If I had to choose between the two, I'm not sure which one I would pick.

"Go ahead," I say, motioning for Mr. Johnson to walk in front of me. "I'm going to hang out in the back with Sage."

Maybe this can finally be the time for Sage and me to talk—and not just because I bartered with my mom.

It's because I miss Sage. And if she's actually giving up the piano to make a point, I'm worried about her.

"Why aren't you up there working on your Pirate's Booty Ball date?" Sage asks me when she catches up.

It feels nice to hear her voice, even if she's being mean.

I put my finger to my lips. "Sage," I whisper. "Please

169

be quiet. This place echoes and Dylan might hear you. And speaking of *that*, what about *your* Pirate's Booty Ball date? I guess I should say congratulations. After all, I only told you that Andrew wanted you, like, two million times."

Sage shakes her head. "I'm not going."

"Root," I call back to her. "Big root." I climb over a fallen log. "Why aren't you going?" I ask, looking back.

Sage hurdles over the log. "Duh! Because I'm grounded," she says. "Do you have amnesia or something? That would actually explain a lot. Maybe you should see a doctor."

"I don't have amnesia, Sage. I thought maybe that something had changed, and we haven't exactly talked much lately."

Especially not after you said I was just like my mom.

Sage is following so close to me that it feels as if she's going to take my shoe off.

"Don't you read my blog?" she asks. She sounds totally serious.

I speed up and ignore her question. "Why did you quit the piano?" I call back.

Sage dredges up and stands by me. "If you read my blog, you would know," she says.

She cuts ahead of me and tries to speed up, but the water is getting deeper, so she can't move as quickly.

I maneuver around some serious cypress roots and catch up to Sage again.

"I've heard you quit in some sort of moral protest against blogging."

Sage turns and gives me a thumbs-up. "You've got it," she says. "*I'm* still completely committed to getting my mom to quit blogging about me, even if you're not. I figure that if I quit the piano, she'll have to see how serious I am—it will have taken only *fifteen* years."

I wonder if maybe Sage is right—maybe the only way to get through to our moms is to take a drastic measure. After all, isn't that what I'm going to do with the Plan?

"Has it changed anything?" I ask, trying to walk side by side with Sage.

"No, she hasn't gotten it," Sage admits as she steps in front of me. "Or not yet, at least. She just thinks I'm being rebellious and trying to hurt her."

"I got my mom to stop blogging about the Pirate's Booty Ball," I say. Even though Sage and I are in a fight, I'm still happy to be talking to her.

She looks back. "How?"

I stop and pause. "I told her I'd talk to you about the piano," I answer softly.

Sage laughs. "That was actually pretty smart, Imogene. This blog thing is changing you. You've finally figured out how to work your mom."

She picks up her speed.

"Thanks, I guess," I mutter, trying to keep up. A week ago, I would've been so excited to tell Sage about the Plan, but not anymore.

I look down and notice that the water keeps rising. I'm trying not to freak out because it's now up to my knees. "What are you going to do if your mom doesn't stop blogging? Are you going to risk your future over it?"

But the piano's more than just Sage's future, it's also what makes Sage *Sage*.

She stops. The gap between the rest of the group and us widens.

Sage digs her walking stick into the ground. "I'm more worried about the here and now," she says. "I'm sick of being my mom's organic guinea pig. Eat this, not that. And I'm sick of hearing about her blog. If she says 'I should blog this' one more time, I'll scream. Barely anyone even reads her blog, by the way—I'm not sure if that makes it better or worse. I'm more than willing to give up the piano for as long as it takes. I know that you've given up on the Mommy Bloggers' Daughters, but I haven't. I believe in it, and I'm going to follow through."

The way Sage says that, I know that we're far from being friends again. I don't think that I've given up on the

Mommy Bloggers' Daughters, but I also don't think it's worth arguing over—at least not in a swamp.

At a minimum, being out in nature has given Sage and me a chance to start talking again. I bet if we hadn't gotten away from school or technology, we would've never had the chance to. And you can't always let your blog talk for you.

"C'mon, stragglers," Raine calls back to us. "Keep up with the group. I have lots of interesting tidbits to tell you about this magical place."

Sage yanks her walking stick out of the water and sets off at a record pace.

"Wait!" I call to Sage. "Are we okay?"

Sage turns around. "Imogene, I get it. You want to do things your way, and I want to do things my way. It's not written in stone that we have to be the same," she says.

"But, Sage, this is about more than the blog," I say. "I'm not sure what's going on with you. The Sage I know wouldn't quit the piano. The Sage I know told me her whole life changed the day she learned to play 'Chopsticks.'"

Sage pauses. "Have you ever thought that maybe we don't know each other as well as you thought we did?" she asks.

She starts trekking back toward the group. I try to keep up, but I trip over a root. I almost fall into the muddy swamp, but I grab on to a strong branch at the very last second.

Sage doesn't look back, not even when I yelp.

Maybe Sage's right about not knowing each other. The Sage I knew would've called out "root."

Mommylicious

"Free-Fallin'"

Dear Readerlicious,

It's Big Question Day, and this one is final *Jeopardy!* hard. At what point do you give up trying to control your kids? Is it when your kids leave the house? Is it when you stop paying for your kids? Is it when they get married?

Or as the parents, are you always the ones in control? Like my mom, Hope, always says, "As long as I'm alive, you'll always be my child." But if we are always someone's child, as long as one of our parents is still alive, when do we grow up?

There's so much I want to tell my daughter, but what should I leave for her to learn on her own? Does every child need at least one heartbreak? If we can protect or advise our children, don't we owe it to them to do so?

Sorry to be such a Debbie Downer today, but we're experiencing some growing pains in our house, and I'm not sure what the best way to handle them is.

To all the mommies out there: How to deal?

In other news, only two weeks to BlogHer! I'm

in serious need of some swag and mommy-blogger power. BlogHer is my personal Christmas morning. I always leave feeling a little bit happier about the world. How about you all?

Butterfly kisses,
Mommylicious

The Mommy Bloggers' Daughters:
The Girl on That Blog

"Going Without"

What's the longest you've gone without eating?

When I was little, I suffered bad stomachaches and had to get my stomach checked out. In order to do this, I had to fast for twenty-four hours.

It was awful.

I got my first computer in the second grade.

My mom was so excited to give it to me.

Like mother, like daughter, she hoped.

I've had two computers since then.

Before last weekend, I don't think I had gone twenty-four hours without using the internet.

But when I did unplug, it wasn't awful at all.

It was great.

The internet is not food.

The internet is not love.

When I checked back on Monday, it took me only ten minutes to catch up on Instagram and fifteen minutes to check my email.

I hadn't missed anything.

Imogene

The Mommy Blogger's Daughter:
Life with VeggieMom

"Life without Music"

The only keys being played in our
house are the ones on the computer.
Sacrifice for what you need.
Sacrifice for privacy.
And, yes, of course, I miss playing
the piano. Silence can be deafening.
VeggieBaby Fights Back

Chapter Thirteen

I JUST SAY YES

MS. HERRING CLAPS HER HANDS THREE TIMES. I THINK SHE'S hoping that we'll clap back like we're still kindergarteners.

"Class!" she says, moaning. "Please be quiet."

I feel bad for her, but it's the last period on Friday, and it's another nice day in Florida. Finally everyone begins to settle down. I wasn't one of the students who was talking anyway.

Who would I talk to?

Sage's still mad at me and is still sitting in the back.

Ardsley and I are friends only when I'm helping her with her blog, which is actually turning out pretty decently the last time I checked it.

And Dylan still makes me nervous, even though he's usually nothing but nice.

"Students," Ms. Herring says. "Today we're going to break into small groups and discuss our blog projects thus far. I know that some of you hear the words 'small groups' and think that you can slack off, but this is not the case. At the end of class, each group will give a mini-presentation on what they've learned from this discussion."

Ever since I started writing more about going unplugged, fewer and fewer people have been interested in my blog. I can't blame them. The Blog Wars were much better fodder for gossip. And despite what I'd hoped, my mom hasn't had a Major Life Revelation since reading about my unplugged idea. In fact, she's glowing with excitement over BlogHer. If anything, she's spending all her time online—or plotting what she'll post about me online next.

Maybe Sage was right to go militant, except I don't think her quitting the piano has changed anything between her and her mom either. She's still grounded and her mom's still blogging.

Basically, I'm back to where I was in the beginning of the year, but without Sage. At least I still have my Plan, capital *P*. It's a last-ditch effort to finally get my mom to listen, but what choice do I have? All my other efforts have epically failed.

Ms. Herring points toward Dylan and me. "You two can be a twosome, and the rest will be groups of three."

Another thing that hasn't changed: I still turn flamingo-pink anytime I'm around Dylan, especially when I'm about to be in a small group with him.

The room goes crazy with screeching noises as everyone drags their desks to be near their small groups.

Dylan and I both turn our desks, so that we're facing each other. I touch my checks, and they feel hot. Awkward.

Ms. Herring circles around the room and passes out a questionnaire to each group.

I look over the questions, occasionally glancing up at Dylan. "Okay. Should we go over these one by one?"

"Sure," Dylan says, but he's looking past me toward the window. It's as if the sun is taunting us.

"'Question one,'" I read. "'Have you learned anything about yourself from having a blog?'"

Dylan laughs. "Yes, I've learned that I hate writing. I never know what to say. Everything I write sounds lame."

I hold up my pen. "Yeah! It's weird to write about yourself," I agree. "I'll put this down: 'We've learned it's really hard to express ourselves in the way we want.'"

Dylan shakes his head. "That's not true. *You're* good at it. It must be in your genes or something."

"Excuse me?" I say without thinking twice. To me, that sounds exactly like when Sage said, "You're just like your mom."

Then it's Dylan's cheeks that turn rosy. "I didn't mean it as a bad thing, Imogene. You just seem much more comfortable with it than I am."

I look over to Sage, who's paired up with Tara and Ardsley. She looks miserable.

I sigh. "It's actually been very hard," I say.

Dylan stretches out his arm on the table. "How so?"

I tap my foot under my desk. "It doesn't matter. Let's keep going. 'Question two: Has your blog affected the way that anyone looks at you?'"

"No," Dylan says immediately. "My parents wouldn't notice if I had a pet hippo in the bathroom. They definitely don't care if I have a blog. What about you?"

I pause. "I think, at first, my blog got attention because people thought I was being brave for writing about my mom. Now I look back and think that I was being stupid. It's not hard to write something online and it's not brave, either. Since I'm no longer writing about issues with my mom, nobody cares about my blog anymore," I say. "People like conflict when it comes to blogs."

Dylan holds up his pen slightly above his paper as if he's confused on what to write down.

"Yes," I clarify. "Yes, it changed the way people thought of me, but not necessarily in any real way. I thought my blog would change things, but it really hasn't."

Dylan stops writing. "I like your blog," he says, looking up at me. "I'm personally into this whole unplugged thing that you're writing about lately. It's very Zen surfer philosophy."

"Really?" I ask. I'm probably turning bird-of-paradise red right now.

"Well, to be honest, I didn't actually like the first posts," Dylan admits. "They seemed like you were always complaining that your mom is involved in your life, but these later posts have been good."

I stop.

"I was complaining about the fact that she's *involved*?" I repeat, gripping the edge of my desk. "You think that my mom has a blog because she's *interested* in me?"

Dylan leans back and puts both his hands behind his head. "Yes. You can't argue against the fact that your mom's interested and invested in your life."

"That's the most ridiculous thing I've ever heard," I say. "She has a blog about me to make money."

Dylan leans forward as if he's challenging me. "Why'd she pick for her blog to be about you, then? Why not cooking or gardening or anything *but* you? If she doesn't care about you, why does she spend so much time thinking and writing about you?"

"You'll never understand," I say. "I'm sorry. Unless you grew up on a blog, you could never understand this."

Sage would understand. Only Sage can understand this, and I don't have her anymore.

"All parents are embarrassing in their own way," Dylan says as if he's some sort of parenting Yoda. He takes the questionnaire from me. "Moving on. 'Question three: Has your blog opened you up to any communities that you weren't previously associated with?'"

I'm able to quell my anger only long enough to get through the rest of the questionnaire and give our mini-presentation on how blogging has changed us.

How could I have ever liked someone who clearly doesn't understand me at all? Any thoughts I had about Dylan liking me—or me liking Dylan—have definitely dissipated.

Another thing blogging has taken from me.

"Imogene!" my mom greets me when I walk in the front door. "I'm sorry I missed your swim meet. I was on an intense conference call about BlogHer."

I toss my swim bag into the laundry room. "No big thing, Mom," I say. "I only broke my own fifty-free record, I think."

"Honey," my mom says. "Let me make it up to you."

"Don't worry about it," I say as I move around her. It's a Friday night and I have absolutely no agenda, but I still definitely don't want my mom making anything up to me.

And why did she miss my meet? Isn't part of the benefits of being a mommy blogger that you get to make your own hours?

First Dylan, now this?

I head up the stairs.

"How about we go to Nordstrom and shop for new BlogHer outfits?" my mom calls.

"Definitely not. No, thank you very much," I call back. I shut my door. I don't want anything to do with BlogAnything right now. Other than working on the Plan, that is.

A few moments later, my mom screams: "Imogene, telephone!"

Who would be calling me? Especially on our house phone? For a moment, I have this delusional fantasy that it's Dylan calling me, and he's planning on apologizing for telling me that it's not a big deal that my mom's a blogger.

For thinking he understands what that's like.

"It's Ardsley Taylor," my mom calls. Even she sounds surprised.

I pick up the house phone.

"Hang up, Mom," I say through the receiver. I sit cross-legged on my bed and wonder what Ardsley is about to say.

"Hi," Ardsley says.

"Hi," I say flatly.

"Imogene," she says, "I'm wondering if you wanted

to come over tonight if you don't already have any plans."

There's a dead silence.

"Why?" I ask.

"What do you mean *why*? Haven't you ever hung out with anyone before? Hanging out doesn't involve a why. It's best without a why. Trust me, I was born to hang out," Ardsley says. I can imagine her making a face at me on the other end.

I stare around my room, contemplating my other options. Read a book? Stare at the ceiling? Think about being friendless?

"Sure," I say. "What time?"

"How about now?"

I pause. I stand up. "Okay," I say.

I took drama in the eighth grade, and I learned that there's one rule in improvisation—and that's that you always have to say yes. Since my life feels like one giant game of improv lately, yes feels like the only thing that I can say.

Chapter Fourteen

TABULA RASA

MY MOM AGREES TO DRIVE ME TO ARDSLEY'S HOUSE. I THINK she's partly doing it in penance for missing my swim meet. My grandma hops in at the last minute because she says she'll go crazy if she stays cooped up in the house a minute longer.

"So . . . ," my mom says. She says *so* in a way that I know she's looking for an opening.

I pull on my seat belt, which is feeling tighter by the second. I turn on the radio.

"Yes, Mother," I say.

She adjusts her grip on the steering wheel. "So . . . ," she repeats.

I twist in my seat and face her. "For someone who writes for a living, you're certainly having trouble finding your words," I comment.

"Yes, spit it out, Meg," Grandma Hope says from the backseat. "At my age, being driven around looks a lot better than shotgun," she adds. "I feel like Miss Daisy from that movie."

"Did you t-talk to Sage?" my mom stutters, her eyes glued on the road. "Ms. Carter is on pins and needles over there. Sage still hasn't touched the piano. She hasn't played a single note since that whole post went viral."

I sit forward and let my seat belt flap. "Yes," I answer. "Or I *tried* to talk to her. I hate to break this to you, but I'm not going to be able to convince Sage to start playing the piano again. But I did try."

Just like I tried to get you to listen to me about your blog, but you didn't. Maybe I'm just not good at being heard, although my mom hasn't written about the dance since the barter—so at least she's sticking to the deal.

Good thing, since there's nothing new to say about the dance. Other than the fact I'm still dateless.

My mom frowns. "It'll all work out with Sage. These hormonal tiffs always resolve themselves eventually."

My grandma Hope coughs from the backseat. "It'll work out if you butt out."

My mom turns around to the backseat. "Maybe *you* should butt out."

Then my mom looks at me, and I realize she's as worried about Sage as I am.

I turn the radio down and wonder if we're finally going to actually talk. About why Sage is so upset. About why I'm so upset. And I wonder if it's all going to happen with my grandma sitting in the backseat.

My mom focuses back on the road. "I didn't know that you and Ardsley were *friends*." She says this in a way so that you know your mom has an opinion and she's trying to get it across without actually saying it.

I should've known that my mom wasn't going to have a real conversation about what we're walking in circles around.

"Weren't *you* always the one that told me that Ardsley would finally grow out of teasing me?" I ask.

My mom nods. "I *was* the one who said that," she says. "Imogene, I'm sincerely glad that you're hanging out with new people, but I want you to know that friends are like CDs."

Grandma Hope gently taps me on the shoulder. "Ah, Imogene, the old record analogy," she interrupts.

"Ardsley's house is up on the left," I interrupt.

My mom moves her foot off the accelerator to the point where the car is barely moving. I can tell she's doing it on purpose. "Imogene, just because you decide you like a new CD, don't throw the other ones away. You never know which ones are going to be classics. You might be taking a break from your favorite CD, but you might want to hear it later."

"What's a CD?" I ask, even though I know what they are—antique mp3s. I sigh. "Mom, if you're trying to tell me to not give up on Sage, listen to me: I'm trying not to."

I don't add that Sage said I was just like my mom, which I'm not, and that it isn't something you just forgive someone for saying. I point out a yellow house on the left side. "We're here."

My mom pulls the car over and I open the door.

"Well, that car ride was more exciting than the Golf Channel," Grandma Hope says.

I turn around and roll my eyes at her.

My mom puts her hand on the door handle. "Should I come in?" she asks.

I quickly hop out of the car. "No," I answer. "Thanks for the ride. See you two at home."

When I'm a few feet from the car, I see my mom hold out her iPhone and click a photo of me walking toward Ardsley's house. And I also see my grandma shaking her head in the backseat.

But of course. At least I still have the Plan. The Plan will have to be what finally gets through to my mom—I only wish it didn't have to come to this.

"Imogene!" Ardsley exclaims when I get to her room. "What you're wearing is, like, such perfection. I die."

I look down. White jeans, a pink tee, and a tiny shell necklace.

"Why is it perfect?" I ask, but Ardsley's already rustling through her walk-in closet—opposed to her annex closet.

Ardsley makes a wand motion with her hand. "You're a tabula rasa of the fashion world, and that's why it's perfect. Duh!" Ardsley answers.

I find a seat on the corner of her bed.

"A *what*?"

"Tabula rasa is Latin for a blank slate. You're my blank slate," Ardsley says. Her voice is chirping with excitement.

Suddenly I feel the same way I felt when my mom told me she got paid for her blog—betrayed. Ardsley hasn't invited me here to hang out—she wants me as her make-over subject. Probably for her blog.

While Ardsley's head is half in the closet, I look out her window to see if my mom's car is still on the street. Nope. She's probably long gone.

"Ardsley . . . ," I start to say as I wonder how I could be so stupid.

Or lonely.

"I don't want a makeover, if that's what you're thinking."

Immediately, Ardsley whips around and gives me a baby pouty face. "But I owe you a favor," she whines. "You've helped me so much with my blog, which, by the way, is quickly becoming one of the coolest things on the entire internet. I need to do something for you in return. It's, like, karma."

I'm pretty sure Ardsley doesn't get the concept of karma.

"I don't want a makeover," I repeat although this isn't exactly true. I prayed all summer for some miraculous back-to-school transformation—both for my looks and for my life. While my life's definitely changed in the past few months, this isn't how I was hoping it would change. And I wanted a physical transformation courtesy of puberty—not Ardsley playing stylist.

Ardsley pulls out a long sequined black dress and lays it flat across the bed. A few sequins catch the overhead light and they twinkle.

"Everyone wants a makeover," Ardsley argues. "Wanting a redo is, like, part of the human condition."

She lays long pearls across the dress.

"And it's not a makeover. It's like a grown-up version of playing dress-up. We can become other people for a night. I'm thinking 1920s silent film stars."

Me, a twenties silent film star? That's a stretch.

I finger the sequins on the dress.

"My mom wore it to some gala in the eighties back when she lived in New York. Now it's part of my collection," she says. "When I get interviewed by *Women's*

Wear Daily, I'm going to mention this piece as an influence for my couture line."

As much as I hate to admit it, Ardsley's passion is infectious. She really believes she can be whoever she sets her mind to being—whether it's a fashion designer or a 1920s film star.

I've never been that confident. The only thing people ever see me as is Babylicious—and she's not even my own creation.

"Please," Ardsley says. "It's either this or E!, and let's face it, we're probably both caught up with the Kardashians."

I remember the only rule of improv is to say yes.

"Fine."

Ardsley shows me a YouTube clip from an old silent film. "See, in silent films, there was always the ingénue and the vamp," Ardsley explains. "Because the films had no spoken words, you had to be able to identify who was who just by their clothes."

I point to the conservatively dressed actress. "Let me guess who I'll be?"

"*Actually*, you're going to the vamp," Ardsley says, and brings up a window with an image of a sultry brunette. "This *is* called dress-up after all."

Ardsley stands up and plugs in hot curlers. "I'll be

wearing my hair in ringlets to make me look more fresh faced. And I'm going to pin yours up in a bob." Ardsley points at a pink velvet love seat in front of a vanity. "Sit here. Just so you know, bobs, or short hair in general, was majorly radical back then."

I sit on the love seat. Ardsley starts shoving bobby pins in my hair.

"You've done a lot of research," I say, watching her and trying not to wince.

Ardsley shrugs. "It's all online," she says. "Can you imagine life before the internet? In the olden days, people had to go to a library just to find something out. Who would ever do that? I would rather just stay stupid."

Sometimes I forget, because I hate blogs so much, that the internet is pretty amazing—it even saves people like Ardsley from giving in to stupid.

After only a few moments, Ardsley has tucked up all my hair with bobby pins. She places a tiny jeweled comb on one side. "Ta-da," she says. "Talk about instant transformation."

I look in the mirror and Ardsley's right. I don't look like Imogene. I don't look like Babylicious, either.

Ardsley winds her own hair into rollers, then gets her computer out and pulls up a Pinterest board of pirate costumes from various movies.

"I'm psyched for the dance," Ardsley says. "I'm going

to do homeless chic meets the original *Peter Pan* look. Tara said I could design her costume too."

I start thinking about the dance. Earlier today I would've given anything for Dylan to ask me to the dance, but now I can't stop thinking about how stupid that was. He actually thinks it's *fun* to have a mommy blogger for a mom.

"Who do you want to ask you?" I ask Ardsley, trying to shake Dylan out of my head.

"I don't want a date," Ardsley declares. "I did want one for a while, but after I started 'Mermaids, Manicures, and Macaroons,' I decided I wanted to go stag. I don't need some guy in a Halloween Express costume messing up my photos. I need high-fashion ones, so I can blog them. My number-one life priority right now is my blog."

Ardsley looks at me and then looks down at the carpet as if she's counting threads. Then finally she looks at me again.

"Hey, I'm sorry I teased you about your mom's blog. It's just I didn't get it . . . until now."

I watch Ardsley's expression. I wait for her to laugh, but she seems sincere, so I just nod.

"That's why I needed to do something for you. I had to thank you because you're the one that helped me get my blog going." She gives me a twirl. "You look glamorous, which is exactly what I was going for. . . . Epic success.

Hey, do you want someone to ask you to the dance?"

"I'm not sure if I'm going," I say. Ardsley raises her eyebrows but doesn't push it.

She holds up the sequined dress. "Put this on," she says. "My hair's nearly set."

I shimmy into the dress and Ardsley carefully zips it. I've never worn anything like this in my life. My mom's closet mostly consists of workout clothes and those are not exactly ideal for dress-up unless you're trying to look like a crazed mommy blogger—which is a little too close to home to be funny.

Once I have the dress on, Ardsley applies a bright red lipstick to my lips—brighter than even Grandma Hope's Ruby Red. I look in the full-length mirror and it's as if my wish has been granted.

For this moment in time, I'm someone else.

I hear a loud whistle. "Wow, I'm good," Ardsley says.

She turns toward the mirror, slips on long white gloves, and covers her shoulders with a tiny fox-fur coat.

Ardsley walks over to the vanity and scrimmages with the objects in the tiny drawer. "You can totally say no this."

"No to what?"

She holds up a tiny pink digital camera. "One picture. For my blog? I want to show off my stylist side."

I nod even though *for my blog* are three of my least

favorite words when put together. I don't want to ruin this for Ardsley. Besides, for the first time in a while, I truly believe that there can be more to me than being Babylicious—even if it is just dress-up.

Chapter Fifteen

YOU'RE GOING TO HAVE TO BRIBE ME WITH MORE THAN PANCAKES

"IMOGENE, WAKE UP," MY MOM SAYS.

I shield my face with my hands. I can never be too careful around her. Who knows if she has a camera?

"Are you wearing lipstick?" my mom asks. She touches her index finger to my lip.

I push her hand away. "Gross, mom. And it was for Ardsley's blog. You can understand that, right?"

I wipe my mouth with the back of my hand. I washed my face after getting home last night, but apparently Ardsley's red lipstick doesn't come off that easily.

"We'll discuss this later, but right now, we're all going out to breakfast. Grandma insists," she says. "Apparently, Grandma Hope's new hobby is family bonding. When I was a kid, she golfed every Saturday morning. But now that *I'm* a busy professional and *she's* injured, she's got nothing but time. *Typical*."

I moan and pull the covers up.

"Mom, can you save it for your blog?"

My mom throws up her hands.

"What happened to my sweet Babylicious?" my mom says.

"She grew up," I say. I get out of bed, walk into the bathroom, and turn on the shower.

"No more makeup, Imogene," my mom calls. "I'm the mother, you're my child, and I have rules."

What about my rules? I think. What about how I want to live *my life*.

"How about you shut down that blog of yours?" I ask, but I've already stepped into the shower so I know she doesn't catch what I said. But she will hear it once the Plan for BlogHer unfolds. She'll hear it—and then some.

The Cove Inn is a historic hotel near the Gulf of Mexico. Actually, it might technically be a motel since all the rooms have their own separate outdoor entrances. The special part about the place isn't the hotel; rather it's the Cove Inn's restaurant—the Coffee Shoppe.

The entire restaurant is smaller than Sage's kitchen, and she lives in a teeny tiny two-bedroom apartment—or at least she did the last time we spoke, which has been a while. All the waitresses have worked here forever. They make Grandma Hope look juvenile.

After we wait forty-five long minutes outside, watching boats dock, we finally sit down. No matter where you sit at the Cove Inn, you're half in the kitchen, since the grill, which is always sizzling, takes up about a fourth of the restaurant.

We all huddle around a folding table with paper placemats. The placemats have a map and illustrations of the waitresses in bikinis—and thankfully, they're all much younger in the illustrations.

"Isn't this terrific?" Grandma Hope asks.

My mom snaps a few photos. "Readers love this place. I can't tell you how many people I've recommended it to. That reminds me: I need to update the Naples section of my website. I should probably get a discount here for all the referrals. Maybe I'll talk to a manager about it."

"How about you do that another time?" Grandma Hope says. My mom glares at her, then turns her camera on me.

"Say cheese!" my mom says, but I hold the menu near my face and block her angle. This is a technique I've learned from *Us Weekly*. It's what celebrities do when they're being attacked by the paparazzi.

And occasionally they also throw punches. I don't

think I'm going to try that.

At least not yet.

"Imogene, you know I'll get a photo of you sooner or later, so decide if you want it before or after you drizzle syrup on your shirt."

Oh, so she *does* still give me choices. And I'm not *that* messy.

I give a little smile.

Click.

My dad flips over his menu on the table. "I'm getting the crepe pancakes with bacon on the side. There's no need to read this."

My dad does this routine every time we come here.

I flip my menu over too. "I'm in," I say.

"Me three," Grandma Hope says. She stacks her menu on top of mine.

I can't help smiling for real, despite my flash-happy mom. Something about the smell of bacon puts me in a good mood—even though I usually have to shower the smell of grease out of my hair after eating here. It's worse than even chlorine.

Our waitress takes our orders and maneuvers around the other waitresses and tables with the poise of a practiced prima ballerina. I've never seen any of the ladies drop a dish or get an order wrong.

I stop watching *The Coffee Shoppe Suite* when I notice

my mom is fishing around in her purse. She pulls out a typed piece of paper and places it in front of me.

"Here's your speech for the BlogHer panel, Imogene," my mom says matter-of-factly.

"You mean, here's *your* speech?" I clarify.

My mom smiles, and I notice my grandma nudge my dad under the table.

"Honey, because you've been so busy with school and your own blog, I thought it'd be easier if I wrote down what you should say. I have a lot more experience with this, and I know that you didn't want to do this panel in the first place. Think of it as an olive branch. We both win."

I look down at the paper. "Starting a Blog: The Advantages of Being a Teen Online."

This is no olive branch. It's not even a twig.

"Have you read my blog lately?" I ask my mom. I try not to raise my voice since this place echoes with the drop of a fork.

My mom nods. "I think your tone's much improved. I know that it's always hard to find a writing voice at first, but this one's so much better."

Find a writing voice? Unlike Mommylicious, my blog's genuine. It's how I feel. It's not a voice—it's me.

"Mom," I say, and look toward my dad and grandma for support. "My blog is currently all about the advantages of taking a step back from social networking. How am I supposed to get up there at the conference and tell everyone how *great* I think blogging is?"

My mom sighs. My grandma signals to our waitress for more coffee. My dad studies his placemat.

"Honey, this is a blogging conference. You can't just get up there and talk about how you think people should unplug. Would that make any sense at all? That's the same as going to a cattle convention and preaching about being a vegetarian. It's ludicrous."

"Meg—" my dad starts to say before my mom interrupts him.

"This is the easy way," my mom says. "You don't have to write a speech since I took care of it for you. I won't even make you thank me."

I quickly look over her speech for me. "Blogging helps me navigate those difficult days at school. Blogging has brought me closer to old friends," it reads.

"Mom, this speech is filled with lies. It's total bullshit," I say. "This isn't what I think at all."

All my life my mom has put words in my mouth and tried to make me into someone I'm not. But today I've finally had enough. I hold the paper up and rip it in half.

"Georgia," my grandma says, looking at me. She takes the two torn pieces of the paper from me and puts them in her purse. She shakes her head at me. "Young ladies shouldn't use that word in polite company." My grandma then turns to my mom. "This *is* bullshit, Meg. I'm old enough to use that word and to call it when I see it."

My dad shakes his head at my mom. "Honey, you shouldn't get to write her speech for her. She's already going out of her way to be on the panel."

"I'm out of here," I say. I push out my chair and walk toward the parking lot. Thank God, I have the Plan. That feels like the only thing saving me right now.

My stomach grumbles for pancakes, but I don't stop walking. My mom might think that she has this whole panel figured out, but little does she know that I've already written my BlogHer speech. I've been fine-tuning it for years. The Plan is so set in motion.

Chapter Sixteen

I WISH MY PARENTS HAD A BLOG ABOUT ME

I'VE WALKED AROUND THE FIFTH STREET AREA ABOUT EIGHT times. I know exactly what Best of Everything is selling in its front window, and I also know that the Starbucks Pumpkin Spice Latte has arrived. I don't feel any calmer. I'm sure that my parents—and my grandma—are out looking for me, but I'm not ready to deal with them right now.

Even though it's only eleven in the morning, I decide to go into the ice cream parlor Kilwins. Right now I'm in serious need of some sort of pick-me-up. As Grandma Hope always says, "Just because you don't buy ice cream from a pharmacist doesn't mean that it's not medicine."

I'm sitting at a table and enjoying my hot-fudge banana "don't judge me" split. As I'm trying *not* to wish I could call Sage to talk over this latest mommy blogger fiasco, the store's door opens and a bell jingles.

Since I don't have a good-luck bone in my body, I turn to see it's Dylan who walks in.

"Tsk. Tsk. Ice cream before noon," he says. "I can't say that I think that sounds good. But what's that saying . . . ? Different strokes for different folks?"

"What are *you* doing here, then?" I ask.

"I decided to change my blog's theme to ice cream," he says. "Dylaneatsicecream.com."

I don't laugh. "I'm not really into blog jokes," I say. "I was previously enjoying a sundae until you appeared. And why are you here if you think ice cream in the morning is gross? Maybe you have some more insightful things to tell me about myself?"

Wow. I've definitely lost my filter this year.

"I'm here running an errand for my mom," Dylan says, lifting his eyebrows. "She's too busy to put my birthday cake order in for next week, so she asked me if I'd do it."

Dylan moves up to the counter where the owner gets out a pad and paper and takes down his order—a mint chocolate chip ice cream cake with Oreo crunch.

Once he's finished paying, I hold my breath for him to leave.

Instead he pulls a chair up to my table, turns it around, and straddles it. I hate it when people sit like that.

"I don't even want to have a family party—or this cake," Dylan says. "My mom and dad will sing 'Happy Birthday' in twenty seconds flat, I'll blow out the candles, they'll take a picture, and then they'll be back on their phones within a minute. The whole thing will be gone and done in ninety seconds. Do you ever hate doing things just because you're supposed to?"

Even though I'm supposed to be acting like I'm mad at Dylan, I find myself nodding. "I feel like half my life I've been playing this role of daughter and my mom's been playing this role of mother, but mostly I feel like it's one big circus for her blog. It's like reality TV, where no one's sure what's real and what isn't."

Dylan makes a firecracker motion with his hand. "News flash, it's like that even if your parents don't have a blog. We're all sort of just pretending," he says. He reaches over and takes my spoon. "Maybe one bite in the morning wouldn't be that bad."

"You're a weirdo," I say, and block him from my ice cream with my hand. "And there is a giant difference between me and you. We're not the same unless your mom has a secret blog about you."

"Have you ever seen *Dr. Phil*?"

I roll my eyes. Is this Dylan's way of telling me that his dream is to be a psychologist and that I'm going to be his first practice patient?

"Yes, I've seen it, but I don't make a habit of watching."

Dr. Phil would have a field day with my mom. Probably me, too.

Dylan looks up, then back at me. "I'm an insomniac," he confesses.

I start to laugh, but Dylan shushes me. "It's a real thing," he says. "I watch a lot of *Dr. Phil* reruns at three in the morning. There was this super-sad episode about a dad who forgot to drop his baby off at day care and he accidently left the baby strapped in its car seat while he went to work. When he realized his mistake, it was too late and the baby had already suffocated in the car's heat."

I put down my spoon. "That's awful," I say.

"It is terrible. The guy was beside himself, so he started a campaign to have parents put a stuffed animal in the passenger seat next to them to remind themselves that their kid is in the backseat of the car."

"That's a good idea, I guess," I say. "I can't really imagine forgetting that your kid's in the car," I add, trying not to sound too judgmental.

Dylan stands up. "That's the big difference between you and me. I can totally imagine it. I think my parents should maybe invest in a stuffed animal."

I can't tell if he's joking.

Maybe it's not just Dylan who doesn't understand me. Maybe I don't fully understand Dylan, either.

I mull over what he's saying. "You think that I'm lucky my mom has a blog about me?" I finally say. "You think that it means she cares about me more than your parents care about you?"

"Your words, not mine," Dylan says. "But, yeah, maybe every once in a while, I wish my parents had a blog about me. At least it would be a daily reminder to me that they knew I was alive." He puts his chair back and makes his way to the door. "By the way, Imogene, I see your parents and your grandma coming this way. I guess they know you pretty well."

Chapter Seventeen

TAKING A MULLIGAN

WITH MY BACK TO THE DOOR, I SIT WITH MY BANANA SPLIT AND just wait for the door's jingle. I try to think of clever things to say to my mom, but my mind keeps going blank. Or back to what Dylan said to me.

I feel a blast of humid air mix with the cool AC. I take a breath and turn around. I relax when I realize only Grandma Hope is walking in.

She smiles and says, "I told your mom that she's done for the day. Finish up your ice cream, Georgia. I'm going to take you to my happy place."

My grandma walks toward the ice cream counter and plucks one of the mini tasting spoons from the bowl. "Actually, I have a better idea. I'll help you finish this. I already blew my diet with those pancakes, so why stop now?"

Silently, we finish the sundae and then I follow Grandma Hope out the door.

"Get in, honey," my grandma says, and nods toward Green Sherbet Delight. "Your parents are walking home. Sometimes I wonder if your mother has a vitamin D deficiency from all that time she spends inside on the computer. Maybe that's why she acts so bananas sometimes. I think some UV rays will do her good."

Once Grandma Hope and I are in the car and are buckled up, she pulls out of her crooked parallel parking job and heads east.

After a few minutes, I have a pretty good idea of where we're going: my grandma's golf club, the Orange Grove. It's one of the oldest clubs in Naples, and they say, "No one gets in unless someone gets out." Grandma Hope says that's a nice way of explaining that the only time someone new can join is when somebody old passes away.

"Grandma Hope!" I scold, and point at her injured wrist. "I know where we're heading, and you're not supposed to play again for over two weeks. Doctor's orders."

My grandma just smiles.

After we pull through the gated entrance, Grandma Hope parks in a spot that has a sign that reads 70+ CLUB CHAMPION, HOPE MATTINGLY.

"It looks pretty neat, right?" she says. "I know that it's not a Hollywood Star or anything, but I'll take it. Probably the next thing that my name will be written on is a tomb-stone, so I'm going to enjoy this. And, Georgia, who in the world said anything about *me* playing?"

She pops her trunk and pulls out her golf clubs. She swings them over her shoulder with such ease that I forget that they aren't actually part of her body. It reminds me of Sage and her fingers on piano keys.

I follow Grandma Hope past the clubhouse to the driving range.

"Fred," she says to an elderly man who's sitting on a stool in a tiny hut filled with buckets of golf balls. "I need a bucket. Hang on, I actually need two buckets, please."

"Anything for you. We've missed seeing you around here," Fred says with a wink. He passes Grandma Hope two buckets.

From her golf bag Grandma Hope pulls out a large driver with a head the size of a small pineapple.

"Georgia," she says. "Here's a driver, some tees, and a bucket of balls. I want you to get on that driving range and just hit the heavens out of these balls—"

"Grandma Hope," I interrupt. "I haven't played golf since three-hole when I was ten years old. You know that it's not my thing. I'm a fish."

She holds out the driver to me, until I finally reach over and take it from her.

"This isn't about golf today," Grandma says. "This is

about frustration. There are certain times when it's good to just come out here and hit the dickens out of some balls. It loosens up something in you." Her eyes are brimming with tears. "That's how I got through your grandpa's passing. I took everything dark in me and put it into hitting the ball as hard I could."

"Okay," I say. "But the ice cream didn't really help, so I doubt that this will either."

While I carry the driver and the golf balls over to an empty spot on the driving range, I try to remember what I learned back in three-hole. Tee up the ball just enough but not too much. Bend your knees. Stick out your butt. Keep your eye on the ball so intensely that you can read its small print.

Before long, I've hit the entire bucket of balls. A few of the swings felt decent. It must be in my genes.

I walk over to Grandma—who's laughing with Fred about something.

"You've definitely got some of Hope in you," Fred says with a nod. "A few of those shots were even keepers."

I smile, because that's definitely a compliment.

Grandma Hope looks me up and down. "You look like you're better. . . . But finish off this second bucket for good measure."

She's right. I do feel better. I almost forgot to think about my mom—and her blog. And the Plan.

It seems like every member of the Orange Grove club—and its staff—stops us, gushes over Grandma Hope, and asks her when she's coming back. When it's just the two of us again, we grab a table on the patio overlooking the putting green.

I watch someone miss the hole by about a centimeter.

"I don't think that putting looks like as much fun as driving," I say, pointing at the golfers at the putting green.

"The driving range is good for getting your frustration out," Grandma Hope says. "But putting is good for when you want to put something out of your mind entirely. If you think of anything but putting, you're going to miss the shot. If you just concentrate hard enough, putting can be like a temporary mind-eraser."

I nod; I've always known that my grandma loved to golf, but I guess that I'm only now understanding why. "It's more than a game," like she always says.

It reminds me of how I feel when I'm swimming. Powerful—and in charge.

"I'm sorry about earlier today," Grandma Hope says after we order nearly all the appetizers off the menu. She leans forward and her pearls dangle above her plate. "Here's my two bits: Your mom was wrong. She shouldn't have written that speech for you."

I take a sip of water and rub my shoulder, which is

already sore. "She doesn't get me at all. I feel like I'm screaming, but I'm trapped underwater."

"I think that misunderstanding might be a family trait," Grandma Hope says. "Does your mom ever talk to you about her golfing?"

"Other than how much she hates it—no," I answer.

The waitress sets down our mozzarella sticks and fries. I should hang out at golf clubs more often.

"She hates it because I forced her to play," Grandma Hope says. She points to a little boy and his dad on the putting green. "That used to be us, except your mom would be crying and stomping all around. It took me until she was in high school to realize that she truly hated golf. I guess I just didn't want to listen—probably because I loved it so much. I wanted it to be something for us to share, but instead it was something that drove us apart."

"Are you saying that my mom is going to come around to how I feel about her blog?"

My grandma laughs. "I don't know. She's pretty passionate about blogging, but I think she will eventually start listening to you. Sometimes, it takes decades for the right words to go through our ears so that we can finally get it. Your mom and I are still finishing conversations we started lifetimes ago. Growing up isn't only hard for kids, Imogene. It's hard for parents, too."

Grandma Hope takes a mozzarella stick off the stack.

"It's funny because, like all moms, I spent years wondering and worrying about what Meg would become. Of course, I never knew to worry about her becoming a blogger."

I shrug. "I guess there are worse things she could've become . . . like a jewel thief or a serial killer," I say.

We laugh, but then my grandma stops and reaches across the table for my hand. "Georgia, have you ever heard of 'taking a mulligan'? It's a golf term."

"Grandma Hope! You know it's been a long time since I took three-hole," I exclaim.

"Okay, okay," she says. "I'm not a fan of this, but taking a mulligan is something some golfers are okay with doing. If someone hits a bad shot, like an 'in the woods, never goin' to see it again' shot, some players let each player take a mulligan and start over with a new ball. Essentially, it's a redo."

I watch my Grandma mentally critique a putter's form.

"I bet that *you* never take mulligans," I say.

"Of course I don't, and I never will, Georgia," Grandma Hope says with a head shake. "I didn't fight with men to create the ladies' league to turn around and start taking mulligans. But I do believe in mulligans in life *off* the golf course."

I squeeze my grandma's hand and then take two fries and place them onto my plate.

"Are you trying to say that I should forgive my mom?"

"I'm not *telling* you anything," Grandma Hope says. "I'm just saying, when it comes to family, *I* believe in mulligans. We all need some mulligans when it comes to relationships. Lord knows that family is a way tougher game than golf."

"I'm sorry that you can't play today," I say. "But thank you for bringing me here."

Grandma Hope leans over and whispers, "Georgia, there are some things better than even golf, but don't repeat me on that. I'll deny it till the bitter end."

I might be willing to give my mom a mulligan for earlier today, but I'm still going through with the Plan, capital *P*. Hitting a few golf balls isn't going to stop me from that.

The Mommy Bloggers' Daughters:
The Girl on That Blog

"It's the End of the Internet . . . and I Feel Fine"

Public Serve Announcement: Have you ever surfed the internet until you can't think of anything else to look at? If yes, try stepping outside for a change. If the elixir of life exists, I doubt you'll find it online.

Unplug: It does a body good.

Skulls and Bones,

Call Me Whatever You Want. . . . I Am Who I Am

PS Hitting golf balls is a great way to unplug.

The Mommy Blogger's Daughter: Life with VeggieMom

"Piano Strikes"

If Gandhi went three weeks without food, I can definitely go two weeks without a piano.

Without all the noise, I'm hoping that my mom can actually hear me.

Mom, no more blogging or force-feeding, please.

If you'd like to find me, I'll be at BlogHer (yes, against my will).

And, yes, I recognize the irony.

Yours Truly,

The Girl Formerly Known as Veggie-Baby

Mommylicious

"The Countdown Is So ON!"

Dear Readerlicious,

"Silent night, Holy night. All is calm, All is bright. . . ." Because it's less than forty-eight hours until BlogHer!

The bag is packed . . . or should I say, the *swag* is packed!

One problem: How am I ever going to sleep tonight?

Readers, have you ever just needed to get away? For me, my blog has always been my best escape. My readers understand me like no one else. While some find solace in a church or a golf course (here's looking at you, Mom), I find my peace with my readers and fellow bloggers at BlogHer!

It nourishes my brain to learn about new blogging techniques and tools, and it replenishes my soul to meet up with like-minded individuals.

"To Blogging and Beyond!" would be my super-hero's motto.

Another great thing about BlogHer is that even though so much changes in our lives, BlogHer is a constant, and it's always a great time.

For those of you going to BlogHer, can't wait to see you. For those of you who can't make it, we'll miss you—and there's always next year.

Butterfly Kisses,

Mommylicious

PS <u>CHECK OUT</u> Imogene's school picture this year. It looks like it was very humid that day. . . . Do they not hand out those tiny combs anymore?

Chapter Eighteen

THE WEATHER'S NOT THE ONLY THING THAT'S FROSTY

MY MOM SHAKES HER HEAD AS WE WALK FROM THE PLANE INTO Terminal C at the Minneapolis Airport. "Thirty-eight degrees in October! That's just inhumane."

Ms. Carter smiles and lets out a sigh. "Home, sweet home. Did you know that we had a blizzard on Halloween in 1991? Twenty-eight, yes, twenty-eight, inches fell. I dressed up as a genie that year. Boy, was that a poor costume choice. Bare midriffs and negative windchill do not mix well. At all."

As we make our way down a series of escalators to the rental-car counter, my mom and Ms. Carter discuss snow, life with it, and life without it. If they've noticed that Sage and I still aren't really talking, they haven't mentioned it.

Maybe they'll blog about it.

I did try to make conversation with Sage on the plane, but she just put on her Skullcandy earphones and ignored me. I can't believe she doesn't even know about the Plan. We used to tell each other everything.

While my mom and Ms. Carter figure out the rental-car logistics, Sage and I sit on a bench—not talking. I see Sage tapping on the metal bench with her left hand. It's the first time I've caught her practicing since she quit the piano. It makes me a little bit sad, but I've learned better than to say anything. Cue the Everglades "You don't know me" moment.

When we get into the rental car, a turquoise Impala, my mom toots the horn three times and nearly startles the Hertz employees to death.

"BlogHer or bust!" she calls out of the ajar window. Ms. Carter lets out an awkward "Whoop, whoop!" They're acting like college kids on spring break—or at least how I imagine college kids on spring break act.

Most of the short car ride to our hotel downtown involves our moms gossiping about how the blogger behind Mommy's Lost Her Mittens is going to show up after her online meltdown, and if the sponsor parties are going to be better than last year's.

At the hotel, check-in is swarming with bloggers carrying bags of swag—that's blog-speak for free party favors.

The swag ranges from sunglasses to washing detergent samples. More junk for our front closet sundry shop.

While in line, my mom turns to Sage and me. "Girls, we have big news. Since you two are growing up, we thought that you young ladies should be allowed to share a room. We know that you don't want to bunk up with your old, boring moms anymore!"

Sage and I exchange looks. We both know that the real reason that our moms are having us share a room is because they want to stay up late drinking Chardonnay with the other mommy bloggers. *And* because they probably think that sharing a room will somehow force Sage and me to become best friends again. Even crazier, they might even think that Sage is miraculously going to decide to start playing the piano again.

But I'm figuring out some things just aren't that easy.

I wish I had a Plan for Sage. At least I have one for the panel.

While our moms meet and greet other bloggers at the opening party, Sage and I sit in the hotel room, eating chicken fingers from room service, and watching a movie on cable.

A year ago, we would've been thrilled to share a hotel room, but not anymore. It's funny how in a few weeks you can go from telling somebody everything to having next to nothing to say to them.

Halfway into the movie, Sage's phone rings and she walks into the bathroom to answer it. I'm sure that it's Andrew, but I don't say anything about it when she comes out.

Not even when her cheeks are all flushed when she returns. I also try not to think about how a part of me wishes Dylan were calling me. He's definitely not going to ask me to the Pirate's Booty Ball after our encounter at the ice cream parlor—and the thing is, I'm not even sure that I want him to. Maybe I misjudged him, too, but that still doesn't mean he should think he knows everything about what my life's like. I've spent *enough* of my life with everyone thinking that they know me.

We finish the movie and Sage turns off the lights. We both lie in our beds, flipping around like chickens roasting on a rotisserie since it's only ten p.m. and we're not actually tired.

Finally I decide to turn my reading light on and look over my notes for tomorrow's panel.

Part of me wishes that I could talk to Sage about the Plan.

But another part of me wishes that Sage wasn't here at all.

I can't change what happened, but I can change tomorrow.

★ ★ ★

"Are you nervous?" Ms. Carter asks me over our hotel's continental breakfast.

I stab a piece of bacon with my fork. "Nope," I lie.

"Sage, aren't you excited for Imogene and Mrs. Luden's panel?"

"Of course," Sage also lies. She pops a mini-muffin into her mouth.

Ms. Carter looks at her disapprovingly.

"Do you know the shelf life of muffins like that one?"

Sage keeps on chewing and picks up another one.

"It's three weeks. Nothing should last three weeks," Ms. Carter says. Her eyes are sparking green fire. "Only *toxins* last three weeks."

My mom smiles and puts her hand over Ms. Carter's: "It's vacation," my mom says, but not unkindly.

Sage holds up her index finger. "This is *not* a vacation," she says.

And I can't help but to nod in agreement, especially when a lady squeals, *"Mommylicious!"* and runs over to our table, nearly knocking a waiter over in the process.

"Hello, group, I'm Biz from BizzyBites, and I'm the moderator of today's awesome panel: 'Mothers and Daughters Who Blog Together Stay Together.'"

The crowd of forty or so, all seated in folding chairs, cheers loudly. Even after a few years coming to BlogHer, it still amazes me that people *pay* to come listen to people talk about blogs.

I'd pay *not* to hear about blogs.

I try to adjust in my seat, but I feel awkward with the crowd watching my every move.

I see two ladies in the third row pointing at me and whispering, and somehow I feel even more self-conscious.

Even though I've grown up in the limelight, it's different here, because 1) this is live and 2) it's not all filtered through my mom. The one good thing is that here, I'm finally in control of how I'm being portrayed.

My mom squeezes my hand and smiles so big you can even see her back molars.

I think that's a clue that she's not satisfied with my smirk, so I grind my teeth and mimic my mom's ridiculous smile.

"On today's panel, we have Meg, the genius behind MommyliciousMeg," BizzyBites announces.

My mom waves to the crowd as if she's on *Miss America*.

The crowd claps and someone yells out, "Mommylicionados for life!"

BizzyBites waits for the crowd to quiet down. "We also have her daughter, Imogene, better known as Babylicious."

Is that who I am better known as? Do I only really matter to people as Babylicious, not Imogene? That thought just fuels my decision to go through with the Plan. I've tried to talk to my mom many times before, but today I'm really going to do it . . . in front of all these people. There's no other way.

My mom elbows me gently, and I give a small, awkward wave. If this were a pageant, I would not win Miss Congeniality.

The crowd claps politely, but this is nothing like the thunder of applause my mom received. Where's my roar? The blog is about *me*, after all.

"And we also have Daughter Knows Best, also known as Patsy, and her mother, Mother Knows Best, also known as Mary Anne."

I look over and decide that Patsy and Mary Anne are identical twins, separated by thirty years. They're even both wearing matching sweatshirts with their blog URLs.

"Each panelist will have a few moments to speak, and we'll also have time for a question-and-answer period afterward," BizzyBites explains.

I look at my stack of papers. On the top, I have the speech that my mom wrote for me. The one I told her I would read if she apologized for writing it without my permission. She *did* apologize, and now she actually thinks I'm going to read it. But underneath it, I have the speech that I'm really going to give. The speech that I wrote back when I thought of the Plan.

Really, it's the speech I've been writing my whole life. It's basically my memoir. Now I just need to be brave enough to see it through.

Looking out into the crowd, I see Ms. Carter sitting in the front row, but I don't find Sage. I can't say that I'm surprised, but it still stings.

"We'll start with Mommylicious," BizzyBites says. "Meg, why don't you tell us about how being a blogger has affected you both as a person and as a mother?"

My mom pauses and leans toward the crowd. She holds up a stack of Mommylicious magnets. "First of all, ladies, I have swag for anyone who's looking for some, and what blogger doesn't love swag? Come and get it after the panel!"

The crowd applauds. My mom is definitely among her people.

"I like to say that I'm a mom first and a blogger second . . . ," my mom starts to say.

As I'm trying to choke back my laughter, I spot Sage sliding into an empty seat in the back. She laughs when my mom says that, and a few ladies in the row in front of her turn, give her a look, and then shush her. I'm surprised that Sage came, but something about her being here calms me down—despite everything that's happened.

My mom continues. "But I also think that being a blogger helps me to be a better mom. I try to live a purposeful life, and I try to share that experience on my blog. I'm always thinking about how I'm going to write something; it's like I have a constant blogging narration going on in my head. I'd like to think that I make my decisions more carefully than I did before I started the blog. And I try to lead a life by example, not just for Imogene—but for my readers, too. I want to be a blog model!"

Sage coughs loudly. I'm happy she's here even if we aren't best friends anymore—even if we aren't friends at all anymore. Her mom's a blogger too, so she'll always understand me in a way that no one else can.

My mom clears her throat and says, "Honestly, I don't think I'd be as good of a mom *without* my blog. When I first became a mother, my blog was what kept me going. If I was worried about something, I'd write a post about it and I'd get the most amazing feedback from my generous readers—many of whom are now my friends."

A few women in the front row wave at my mom. She winks back at them.

"I'm happy to say that a few of those readers are even here today; they've stuck with me throughout the years. In the olden days, people had tighter-knit communities, and they could rely on the people around them. Nowadays people are more scattered, but the internet, especially blogging communities, helps to fill that void. Blogs are powerful. We are powerful," my mom says.

I feel like I've heard this speech a thousand times. I turn my focus to channeling my courage. After fifteen years, I'm finally going to tell my mom how I feel. The Plan is on.

My mom pauses and clears her throat. She grips the folding table with one hand and takes a deep breath.

"I've never actually told anyone this before, but I was diagnosed with pretty serious postpartum depression after Imogene was born. There were days when I didn't know where to turn. I thought I'd like being a stay-at-home mom, but I was lonely and confused. The blogging community saved me," she says.

She wipes a genuine tear from her eye. I turn all the way toward my mom—startled by this confession. I never knew any of this.

The audience claps and leans in. Like them, I'm waiting to hear what she'll say next—and for the first time in a long time, I'm going to try to listen.

It's like what Grandma Hope said: "Sometimes it takes decades for the right words to reach our ears." My mom's blog might have evolved into some kind of monster, but I never actually thought much about why she started it in the first place. I still don't want her writing about me, but I realize that she didn't create the blog to harass me. She created the blog as a life raft for herself—for the both of us. But why couldn't she have told me about all this in private? Why is everything always public with her?

My mom starts speaking again. "Thank you all for being such an amazing community. I'm not sure who I'd be without y'all. And now, I'm going to pass the proverbial baton, or the proverbial mouse in our blog lingo, to my daughter, who started her very own blog this year."

I look at my mom, and she's smiling and wiping her tears with a Kleenex someone from the audience passed up.

I can see why she loves BlogHer. Here, she is a happy, popular blogger among friends and fans—even if her own daughter isn't one of them. If she helps hundreds, even thousands, of people and the blog helps *her*, who am I to put a stop to that?

But can I continue to live life like this, in the shadow of Babylicious?

"Thanks for that amazing talk, Mommylicious," BizzyBites says as she pushes the microphone toward me. "Babylicious, the floor is now yours."

I look at Sage, and I swear she nods at me. Even after everything, I know that she's still here for me in her own way. Maybe that's what she was trying to tell me in the Everglades—that it's okay for both of us to choose our own paths.

Then I look down again at both speeches, and I decide that I'm not going to read *either* of them. I can't embarrass my mom in front of all her friends. This isn't the right place to get through to her. The Plan is off.

I breathe in and begin. "Hi, everyone! I'm Imogene. Some people out there might think that my real name is Babylicious, but—it's not. I actually checked my birth certificate once to make sure. My actual name is Imogene Georgia Luden, and I had a speech all prepared for you today. Actually, I had two speeches, but now I'm not going to read either of them. In you-people speak, I'm hitting the delete all button and I'm now free-writing."

The crowd hushes as if something actually major has just happened. Maybe it has—at least for me.

I look toward Sage and she gives me a thumbs-up. I don't know if she agrees with what I'm saying, but I like knowing that she's here for me right now.

"To be honest with you all, I've wished for my entire life that my mom had chosen a different career. I even used to clip HELP WANTED ads from the newspaper and leave them on the kitchen table for my mom to see. And while I'll admit I'm very tired of being her model *and* subject, I know that if I ever get amnesia, I will at least have her blog to help me remember the past fifteen years. I'll be especially glad to relive my first period."

The crowd laughs and my mom even lets out a small chuckle. I hold up my hand and continue.

"But in all seriousness, I want everyone here to know that my mom's success isn't magic. To have a popular blog like my mom's, you also have to be extremely dedicated. It's not something that just happens overnight. She works all the time on her blog. I have a blog now too, and I also know that what you post affects people. You have to really be strong to put up with the criticism. Sitting here in front of my mom's fans, I understand why she works so hard at her blog and that's because it matters to a lot of people. Because of that, I'm proud of her."

I look at my mom. "Thank you very much for having me here today. I learned a lot."

The crowd claps softly as I pass the mic.

I study my mom and I try to gauge her face. Is she mad that I didn't read the speech she wrote? Or is she confused over what my other speech was going to be? But I don't see any anger in her face.

Even though I didn't go through with my Plan to read my speech that ripped into her, I still feel a sense of relief. Maybe the Plan wasn't such a good idea after all.

She whispers in my ear, "Thank you for that. That was way better than the speech I wrote for you. It had more heart."

I smile back at her.

We meet up with Ms. Carter and Sage in the hotel restaurant after our panel.

"Thanks for coming to the panel," I tell Sage. "I have a gift for you." I place a large rainbow cookie I bought from Starbucks in front of her.

Sage looks at Ms. Carter, who shrugs. "It's vacation," she says. "Or, at least, it's vacation for me. I just love BlogHer. So many positive vibes. It's like one giant rock crystal. Talk about good energy. And you ladies were just *great*. Especially with that impromptu speech, Imogene."

"Thanks, Imogene," Sage says just before taking a huge bite. She covers her mouth and mumbles, "You didn't have to do this."

"And you didn't have to come to the panel," I say.

Our moms smile at each other. I smile too. Maybe this is what rebuilding a friendship is like. One cookie at a time, if your friend is Sage.

"What was that other speech you mentioned, Imogene?" my mom asks me. "I'm just curious."

Sage looks at me.

"I'll give you that speech some other time," I say. "I've been practicing it for a few years now. It's not something I needed to say in front of your fans. It should be private. I know that's a dirty word for bloggers, but some things are personal, and my speech is one of those things."

Ms. Carter raises her eyebrows and gives my mom a look, but my mom turns to me and nods.

"Okay, we don't have to talk about it here or now, but I'm making sure that you tell me about it soon."

Chapter Nineteen

THOSE SMALL MOMENTS

AS I'M PACKING UP MY BAG AND TRYING TO GET IT TO ZIP despite the bulge that the swag is making, I think about how BlogHer actually went okay. Sage and I attended a few events with our moms. I posed for a dozen pictures with readers, and I tried *really* hard to use my genuine smile. I even got some fashion bloggers' contact information for Ardsley. Just because I'm not into blogging doesn't mean I shouldn't help out a friend—or something like that.

I've spent so much time worrying that people wouldn't think there was more to me than Babylicious that I forgot that people are *always* going to see you differently from how you actually are. But the ones who count will stick around and get to know you beyond appearances—or the online character your mother's created out of you.

I hear a *knock, knock* at the door.

"Imogene, are you ready?" my mom says. "Everyone else has been waiting in the lobby for five minutes."

I push down on the suitcase hard, and it eventually closes just enough to zip.

"Yup," I say. "I'm ready."

Downstairs, Sage and her mom are already sitting in our rental car. My mom and I put our luggage into the trunk and slide into the car.

Ms. Carter starts driving toward the highway. At a stoplight, she pauses a moment before she turns the wheel sharply and executes a U-turn.

"Where are you going?" my mom asks. "Did you forget something? That sign back there said that the airport is the other way."

Ms. Carter shrugs and points at the clock. "We've got a lot of extra time." She motions to the road down on the right. "That's my old street coming up. I want to show you guys where I grew up and where Sage was born."

Sage rolls her eyes.

I feel sorry that Sage and her mom still aren't getting along—at all. I know exactly what that's like. I can't believe it, but I actually *am* grateful for our panel. And happy I didn't have to go through with the Plan.

As we drive down the street, I try not to fixate on how run-down and poor the neighborhood looks. Most of the houses are one-story and teeny tiny, and nearly all of them need a paint job. Outside some of the big apartment buildings, people stand around, even though it's freezing out—like see-your-breath cold. I try not to notice when my mom presses down on her door's lock.

"Is this where I was born?" Sage asks. Sage moved to Florida at four years old. She says that her only vivid memories of Minnesota involve making snow angels, putting on and taking off her snow boots and mittens, and riding a log flume at the Mall of America.

"Yes," Ms. Carter says. "We're almost to our old place."

Ms. Carter slows down and pulls in front of a one-story house with chipped paint. There's a rusty chain-link fence and a KEEP OUT sign in the wild lawn.

Ms. Carter pulls out her iPhone and takes a few pictures through the car window. She frowns for a brief second. "It's sad seeing how they let the place go. I have lots of great memories from there."

"It looks like they let the *whole* neighborhood go," Sage comments with wide eyes.

Ms. Carter shakes her head. "No, the neighborhood has been like this since I was a little kid. It's always been a little rough around the edges. We always kept our house up, though."

Ms. Carter puts the car back into drive, and we start down the street again.

"A little rough around the edges?" Sage asks with her nose firmly at the window. "This place makes our neighborhood look like Disney World."

"That's *why* we moved to Florida, Sage," Ms. Carter says. "It *is* Disney World compared to this neighborhood. The schools are better, and there's half the crime. Why did you think we moved there?"

"The weather?" Sage answers sincerely. "Maybe the beach? Something about it being more organically in tune? I don't know. I was little. . . . I never really thought about it."

Ms. Carter smiles and says, "Actually, I liked the seasons here. There's something nice about change four times a year. And while Minnesota doesn't have the Gulf of Mexico, it does have over ten thousand lakes."

Sage is quiet as we continue out of the neighborhood. Just before the entrance to the highway, there's a large tan building with a blue cross hanging over the front door. Sage points to it. "I remember that place. I know that I remember it," she says softly.

Outside of the building, snaking around a corner, is a long line of people.

"Is that a church?" I ask, pointing out the window.

Ms. Carter slows the car. For a second I think she's going for her phone to take a picture. Instead she pulls over to the side of the road.

She pauses before answering. "It's shelter and a food bank. Those people are waiting for a Sunday meal. They also have temporary apartments for families in need or crisis."

"We lived there," Sage says softly.

Ms. Carter nods. She turns around and looks at Sage. "For a little while we did. I'm sorry, Sage. I didn't mean to bring us this way. I must have forgotten it was this direction. It's a great place that does very kind things, but it's not where we had some of our best memories."

My mom reaches over and rubs Ms. Carter's shoulder.

"It's okay," Sage says. "I'm glad we came this way."

My mom and I are quiet. I feel like an intruder in a moment that doesn't belong to me. For big events like weddings and funerals, guests are usually invited, but sometimes it's the small, private moments that really change people. It seems strange to be an audience to one of those moments. It's as if I can almost feel something changing between Sage and her mom.

It's sort of how it felt for me yesterday at the panel.

Without another word, we drive to the airport.

"You're home!" calls out Grandma Hope as we open the front door. "How was the Midwest? Any Paul Bunyan sightings?"

"You're upstairs!" my mom says.

"Yes," Grandma Hope says. "I was just spending some time with my favorite son-in-law. He needed some extra hands—rather, one extra hand—for a project he's been working on."

"I'd like kisses from my ladies," my dad says. He's sitting at the kitchen table and has thrown a tarp over whatever he was working on.

"Go on," Grandma Hope says. "Don't leave the man waiting."

Both my mom and I go over and give my dad a kiss on the cheek.

"Thank you," he says. "I see that you're *both* alive. Hope, you lost the bet and you owe me fifty dollaroos. Please pay up in a timely fashion."

My grandma laughs, but I'm not entirely certain it's actually a joke.

"How did it go?" my dad says. "Maybe next year I can come to this meeting of the bloggers. It sounds like something out of a Roald Dahl book."

My mom pulls up a chair and sits next to my dad.

"You would've been really proud of Imogene," she says. "Your daughter gave a great speech."

Grandma Hope also pulls up a chair. "I take it that means she didn't read the one you wrote *for* her, Meg."

My mom lets out a fake cackle. "You're hilarious, Mom. No, Imogene did the speech impromptu. It was very touching. I know that she says she doesn't want to be a blogger, but she does have a gift with words."

"If you all don't mind, I'm going to go upstairs and have a few blog-free moments," I say. "I also need to get under the covers and warm up. I'm still freezing from Minneapolis."

My mom walks up to me and warms me up with her hands like she used to when I was little and got into a cold bed. "See you tomorrow," she says. "I'm still holding you to your promise about your other speech."

I head up to my bedroom. I practice my newest speech, one that I worked on during the flight. I still get my message across in it like I did in one from the Plan, but it's not so angry. For once, I'm not scared or mad, I'm just ready.

Chapter Twenty
I'VE WAITED A DECADE TO TELL YOU THIS

"MOM," I ASK, "CAN I STAY HOME FROM SCHOOL? I'M BEAT from our trip."

Staying home from school used to be my favorite thing ever. I'd drink orange soda and watch *The Price Is Right* and daytime soaps. As I got older, I stopped asking to stay home from school because that was the only time I knew that I was free from my mom and her blog.

But today's different.

My mom turns around from stirring her pot of oatmeal.

"I'm doing fine in all my classes, and I can miss one day. I promise," I say. "Besides, we have a lot to talk about—like my other speech."

My mom grabs a bowl from the cabinet and dishes out a helping. She sets it on the counter.

She pulls up a stool. "Okay, but can I have breakfast first?"

"Sure," I say. "Nobody should ever talk about the big stuff without a full stomach." Dad's words, not mine.

After my mom and I finish breakfast, we sit in our family room. I'm happy not to be having another living-room talk. That was scary. I felt like I was on *Downton Abbey*.

"Mom . . . ," I start to say. "You know how when you write your blog, you just write it and people can only make comments afterward?"

"Yes." Mom raises her eyebrows only a little bit.

"Can this work the same way? Can I say everything I need to say and then you can comment afterward?"

My mom puts her hand over mine. "Of course. I'm always willing to hear what you have to say."

I know that she's a good mom and that she probably does mean it, but I also know that sometimes it's hard to listen when someone's going to tell you something you don't want to hear.

"I've been practicing and revising this for a long time," I say. I pinch the couch's leather between my fingers and squeeze hard. "I don't want to be the focus of your blog anymore. I know that your blog means a lot to you, and after this weekend, I understand why you started it in the first place."

I breathe in. I can't look at my mom, or I know that I won't be able to keep going. "I understand that you started it because you wanted to grow as a mother and as a person, and I think that the blog is an important part of who you are."

"It is."

I put my finger to my lips and continue. "I'm not asking you to stop writing or to stop blogging, I'm just asking you to stop writing about *me* online. Whether I like it or not, most people spend a lot of time online and what people write online does count. It stays online and it's going to be around even after you're not—"

"That's morbid," my mom interrupts but then stops herself. "Okay, I'll be quiet."

"When you write about me online, I feel like I'm losing part of myself. I'm scared to do anything, because I'm worried you're going to blog about it. I can honestly say that I understand why Britney Spears went 'bald-head, umbrella-wielding' crazy. Sometimes people need to make their own mistakes and live their own lives without people watching or commenting on it every five seconds. Once in a while I want to have a bad hair day and not have to worry about you blogging about it."

My mom nods.

"I know that you'll always have an opinion, and I'm okay with that, but I want you to share your opinion with me—not the World Wide Web."

My mom frowns.

"I want to choose a college without hearing any of your readers' thoughts about it. I want to choose a boyfriend without reading about it online. I want to finish growing up *without* you blogging about me," I say. "Actually, I think I can only grow up when Mommylicious—and Babylicious—sign off."

"I do it because I love you," my mom squeaks out. Tears fall from her eyes, and they splatter the couch like rain on a windshield.

I hand my mom a Kleenex.

"I know that's why you started it," I say. "But I'm asking you for my privacy. And I want you here in the present. I can tell when you're writing your blog in your head. Your mouth actually moves. It's like you're trying to shape our lives through your writing and your pictures. I don't want that, Mom. I want us to just enjoy this time in real time. I don't want you to hide behind your blog anymore."

"I'm sorry you feel this way," my mom says. "I'm sorry that my blog blinded me from seeing how you really feel."

I move to hug my mom, and I realize I don't have much else to say.

"Just think about it, please," I say.

My mom nods. "I'll do that, Imogene. Thank you for telling me how you feel—I know that isn't always easy for you."

I spend the rest of the day drinking orange soda and catching up on *Days of Our Lives*. When I hear the doorbell, I get up off the couch to answer it. I look through our peephole and hesitate before opening the door.

It's Dylan. He looks as handsome as ever, wearing neon board shorts and carrying his skateboard.

"Hi," I say, but I don't welcome him in. I'm still a little annoyed by how he acted at the ice cream parlor.

He pulls a sheet of paper from his backpack. "Algebra homework," he says. "I noticed you weren't in math class, so I skateboarded over to drop this off."

I put the paper down on our entryway table. "How thoughtful. I was *just* thinking to myself a few moments ago that I wished I were doing the quadratic equation."

"Sarcasm," he says, nodding. "I like it. You don't look sick, by the way."

I shake my head and wave him in. "I'm not. It's called a personal day. I'm recovering from the blogging convention."

He sets his skateboard down in the entryway, and we

wander toward my kitchen.

"Was it that bad of a weekend?" Dylan asks.

"No, it was okay," I say, smiling big. "I actually had an epiphany, and realized how darn lucky I am to have a mom who blogs about my every move."

"Touchdown: sarcasm," Dylan says in a sports-announcer voice. "Listen, I'm sorry if I offended you at the ice cream parlor—and in English class."

I open our fridge and toss Dylan a water bottle.

"You didn't," I say. "You're entitled to your opinion."

Dylan chugs half the bottle with one gulp. He sets it down on the counter.

"I was pissed at my parents," he says. "I've been annoyed at them all year. They keep making promises and breaking them, and then they try to bribe me by letting me have parties. I guess I was just jealous. Your family is so *Brady Bunch*."

I raise my eyebrows.

"Fine, *Modern Family*," he says. "You guys are always together. I bet you couldn't even pick my dad out of a crowd."

"Thanks for the homework, I guess," I say. "And I am sorry your parents aren't around more. Maybe you should talk to them. I think parents are sometimes just clueless about how their kids are actually feeling."

Dylan sighs. "Do you know that you're much better than the weird shrink my parents sent me to in elementary school?"

"Thanks," I say. "Hey, have you ever thought about writing a blog about your parents? *That'll* get their attention. Believe me, they'll notice, although I don't recommend it at all. Grounding usually ensues."

Dylan laughs. "Hey, Imogene, what about that Pirate's Booty Ball thing?"

"What about it?" I say. I know I'm turning lifeguard-swimsuit red.

He looks down at his shoes. "Would you be interested in going with me?"

I've been waiting for Dylan—or anyone—to ask me that for so long, but I never thought it would happen like this.

"Of course I'll go with you," I say. "But I'll only go as long as we promise *not* to talk about our parents. Or about blogs."

Dylan reaches over for my hand to shake on it. "Deal. And I've thought about it, Imogene, and I understand that there are some good reasons why you don't like your mom blogging about you. Namely, that you feel stalked and manipulated by her. I'm sorry I didn't see that before. I was only thinking of my own situation."

I shake my head. "It's okay, Dylan. I also need to remember the reason she started the blog in the first place. You were right. It does come from a good spot."

I walk Dylan to the door. Just as I'm opening it for him, my mom stumbles in with two bags of groceries.

"Hi, Dylan," she says in a startled voice.

I watch her eyes go to her camera, which is sitting right next to my algebra worksheet.

She catches my eye, and she pauses. "I hope I'll see you around soon. Have a good night." She shuts the door behind him.

I nearly cry with happiness.

No *click*.

My mom opens her mouth and then shuts it. "I'll unpack these, and I won't ask you why Dylan was here. I'll try that privacy thing."

But for once in my life, I want to share my news with my mom. And I'm only mildly worried that she'll share it with the World Wide Web. But after my talk, maybe she won't.

"Guess what?" I say. "Dylan asked me to the dance. Well, technically, he asked his shoe, but I think he meant me."

My mom squeals and gives me a big hug.

I run upstairs to scream into my pillow.

Later that night I'm on my bed, working on my newest blog entry, when my phone vibrates.

It's a text from Sage.

Sage: U aren't anything like ur mom. I'm sorry.

Me: I know. I'm your best friend, after all.

Sage: Hope u feel better—but I don't think u were really sick. ☺ PS U r nothing like Babylicious. You're MUCH cooler. C U in front of school tmrw?

Me: Definitely. & . . . I want u to be the 1st to know that Dylan asked me to the dance!! Wish u weren't grounded.

Maybe Sage and I do both know each other just as well as we thought—and we've also let each other change, which is probably the greatest gift you can give to a friend.

Chapter Twenty-One

THE PIRATE'S BOOTY BALL

OF COURSE, THE OFFICIAL NAME OF THE DANCE ISN'T PIRATE'S Booty Ball. Father Sullivan would definitely *not* go for that. The official name of the dance is the Pirate's Ball, but among the ninth graders, it has *always* been called the Pirate's Booty Ball.

After I lace up my knee-high pleather boots over my fishnet stockings, I take a look in the mirror. Dressed in a red-and-white-striped raggedy wench's dress, complete with a pirate's hat, I don't look anything like myself. Obviously, I'm in costume, but something else is different. I feel like I'm missing something, and I know that it's Sage. What's a wench without her best friend?

I wish she wasn't still grounded and could come to the dance.

"Imogene! Your date is here!" my mom calls. Her voice sounds like a teenager going gaga for a teen idol. I brace myself for the photos that are about to happen. Even though my mom's promised to "evolve" her blog, she's still definitely going to take a thousand photos—even if they're just for her.

After all, she still has photo rights to the dance per our barter.

I take a few breaths and walk down the stairs.

"Arrrrrgh!" Dylan calls.

I laugh. I used to think Dylan was the coolest guy ever. Now I realize he's a total dork, which just makes me like him more. I guess just as there's more to me than Babylicious, there's also more to Dylan than looking like a model on a Florida postcard.

Dylan takes his plastic sword out of his holder and poses for a solo shot.

"Am I going to be on the blog?" he asks as my mom snaps away.

"I'm afraid not," my mom says, and winks at me.

Dylan turns toward me, raising his eyebrows.

The door from the basement swings open, and Grandma Hope walks in, panting from running up the stairs.

"Goodness!" she says between deep breaths. "I wouldn't want to have missed this, but I was tied up on the phone signing up for a computer class. I figured it's about time. I'm officially going to join the gaggle of Google."

Now it's my mom who's raising her eyebrows. *"Really?"*

"Really," Grandma Hope answers.

I've always loved how great my grandma is at golf, but it's also been great to see her embrace other things these past few weeks. She's one brave Ace.

"Hello, Dylan," my grandma says.

"Hello, Grandma Hope," Dylan says.

"Please excuse my manners." Grandma Hope pulls out a tube of eyeliner from behind her back. She holds it up to my mom.

My mom nods. "Go on, but *just for tonight*, Imogene. . . ." She holds up her index finger. "The makeup ban is only lifted for tonight. You might not be a baby anymore, but I'm still your mother."

Grandma Hope mock-wipes sweat off her eyebrow. "Thank goodness." She walks a few steps over to me and with her good hand, she applies a thin coat of eyeliner. "Perfect."

I check out my reflection. *Not bad.*

Grandma Hope holds up a tube of mascara.

My mom shakes her head at my grandma. "Don't push it, Mom."

"What about you Dylan?" Grandma Hope asks, heading in his direction with the eyeliner in hand. "That

Johnny Depp pirate makes guy eyeliner look pretty hand-some if I do say so. I'm not a cheetah or anything, but he's not bad on the eye."

"It's called a cougar," my mom says, laughing. "Old ladies who go after young men are *cougars*. And if they're *really* old—not that you are—they're called jaguars."

"This is why I need this Google thing. Then I won't have to take your word for it all the time," Grandma Hope says.

My grandma reaches Dylan and he quickly puts his hand over his face. "No, thank you!" he squeaks.

Just then my dad emerges from the kitchen covered in tiny woodchips. "Hello, Dylan. Do I have your pirate's honor that you'll take good care of my daughter tonight?"

"Sir," Dylan says mock-seriously. "Pirates aren't par-ticularly known for their honor, but I'll take great care of Imogene."

A few months ago, I would've been mortified by all this, but I'm realizing part of the fun part of life is peeling back layers and showing people your real life, even if that includes a photo-happy mom, a golf-fanatic grandma, and a corny, messy dad. Dylan's also helped me to realize that I actually have a pretty cool family—even if my mom *is* a mommy blogger.

I'm much happier with Dylan witnessing my real life rather than just reading about me on a blog.

After a few dozen pictures in several different configurations, my mom finally says, "It's a wrap."

We're nearly to the door when my dad calls out, "Wait!"

"What, Dad?" I say. "We've got to go! We don't want to miss the boat."

After my dad laughs at my corny joke (I guess it runs in the family), he goes to a corner of the living room where there's a tarp laid over something. He takes it off and reveals a piece of driftwood. "I wanted to show this to you both." He holds it up. He's removed all the barnacles and, in tiny seashells, it spells out "Imogene."

"It's for your room," my dad says, holding it up like a trophy. "I'm thinking about selling my woodwork on that Etsy website. I like doing this nearly as much as I like doing my work for my job," he says.

I walk over to inspect Dad's piece. It really is beautiful. "Thanks, Dad. I love it."

"That's so cool," Dylan says, coming over next to me to look. "Maybe I'll order one. It's very surfer, and my mom's been asking me if I want to redo my room."

My dad nods toward my mom. "See, honey, I've already got my first customer. We'll be rich in no time."

I give my family a last smile, thinking how these milestones mean just as much to your family as they do to you.

And even though it's annoying that they take a million pictures, they're usually just doing it because they love you.

"Dylan, over here!" I hear a man's voice say. We're just about to enter the school gym, where the dance is being held.

Dylan and I turn toward the sound and a flash nearly blinds us.

"Mom? Dad?" Dylan says, rubbing his eyes.

"Surprise! We're chaperones for the night," Dylan's mom says, holding up a very fancy camera. She's wearing a Lilly Pulitzer maxi dress, but she's also wearing an eye patch. She points at it. "I even dressed up for the party!"

Dylan's dad is wearing a linen suit. He's just as handsome as Dylan, but in an old-man way. "I came from work," he says, looking down as his clothes. "But I used to be the master of a costume party."

I look at Dylan, and he starts laughing, which makes me start laughing.

"Thanks for coming," he says. "Maybe next time give me a heads-up."

"We wanted to surprise you," his mom says, snapping another photo. "Imogene, pose with your pirate," she says.

I stand arm in arm with Dylan, thinking how it's not

only famous bloggers who embarrass their kids. It's all parents.

"Okay, we're heading for punch-bowl duty," Dylan's dad says. He does a few disco moves through the doors and Dylan covers his face.

"Totally embarrassing," he mutters, but then he smiles a bit.

He must have talked to them, I think, but I don't say anything. I just smile back.

Even though the doors are closed, I can still hear the Carly Rae Jepsen lyrics blasting through them.

"Are you ready for me to embarrass you on the dance floor?" Dylan asks.

I hesitate.

"Imogene, I'm just joking. I'm not as bad as my dad," Dylan says. He does a little amateur moonwalking to prove his point. He dances forward and stops at my toes. He looks into my eyes.

"Something's wrong," he says. "I can tell."

"It's just . . . ," I start to say.

"Sage isn't here," Dylan answers for me.

I nod.

"Wait here, Imogene," Dylan says, and then walks into the gym.

Ardsley and Tara strut toward the gym's doors. They're

dressed identically, both wearing pirate costumes that look more runway couture than Halloween surplus store.

"I like your costumes," I say.

They smile at me and strike a pose. And then another pose. And another.

"You're going to get tons of blog action when you post photos of this, Ardsley," I add.

"Imogene!" Ardsley squeals. "Do you *really* think so? I spent a lifetime designing them. And guess what? I got three emails from these, like, real fashion bloggers saying that they love my blog, so an epic *thank-you* for helping me. And double guess what? Someone from Indonesia looked at my site. I don't even know where that is, but I'm going totally global. Next stop, *Paris!*" she says in a French accent.

I smile at Ardsley. Even though I'm technically against blogging everything, I realize now that it's not one of those black-and-white deals. For some people, blogging is like medicine. I prefer ice cream, but it's all personal taste— unless your blog is about someone else, who doesn't want to be written about. Then you should reread my speech.

"Imogene, can you take our photo for my blog?" Ardsley asks, passing me her cell phone.

Tara and Ardsley start posing like runway models again. I've snapped about a dozen shots. I'm handing

Ardsley her camera back when Dylan and Andrew return from the gym.

"Toodles!" Ardsley calls as she heads through the open doors. "See you in there!"

"Toodles!" I say back. Maybe it's not such a terrible word, after all. It's got a certain charm to it.

"I've got a thought," Andrew says. He points toward the school's front entrance.

"I think I've got the same one," I say, and lead the way out.

It's Halloween night, so there's some major pedestrian traffic.

A few parents walking around with their kids give us serious "Aren't you too old for trick-or-treating?" looks, but we just march onward. Three pirates on a mission.

Once we're finally at Sage's door, I say, "Here's hoping."

Andrew rings the bell.

A guy with a black goatee answers the door. He must be the orange farmer.

He holds up a bowl of plastic bags with dried fruit in front of us. "Aren't you supposed to say 'trick or treat'?" he asks. "I'm pretty sure that's part of the getting candy deal."

"*That's* not candy, and we're not here to trick-or-treat,"

I answer. "May we speak to Sage?"

"Sure," he says with a smile. "Come on in."

The three of us walk into Sage's apartment. The kitchen counter is filled with tons of jars, and it smells sweet and fruity. It must be one of Ms. Carter's vegan projects.

Sage and her mom are sitting on the couch, watching *It's the Great Pumpkin, Charlie Brown* on TV. When the door shuts, Sage turns around and sees us—an awkward trio of pirates in her living room.

"Why aren't you guys at the dance?" she asks. She's dressed in a pair of leggings and a purple tunic.

"Because you weren't," I answer.

I turn to Ms. Carter. "I know you aren't happy that Sage still isn't playing the piano and that you two are working on some things, but please let Sage come to the dance. It doesn't feel right for her not to be there."

"I concur with everything Imogene is saying," Andrew says.

"Whatever they say," Dylan agrees.

Ms. Carter balls her fists. "Sage is too good to just quit." She shakes her head. "I can't stand by and watch that."

I give Ms. Carter a small—but real—smile. I do think most moms do mean well, but I also think moms often mix up what's best for them and what's best for *us*.

Ms. Carter sighs. "All right, I guess it's up to Sage. She can go to the dance if she wants to, but she's technically still grounded until she starts playing the piano again."

"Sage?" I ask. I know that I'm asking more than just if she wants to come to the dance. I'm asking her if she wants to be best friends again. We've both changed a lot this year, but I still need her as my best friend. She's a classic—just like my mom said.

"Yes, I'll come!" she squeals without missing a beat.

Andrew takes his pirate's hat off his head and places it on Sage's. "Insta-costume," he says.

I can see why Sage likes him—he's a sweetheart.

Then we all race for the door, as if, at any moment, we'll turn into pumpkins. Maybe that's what being a teenager feels like . . . a race to live before you turn into a pumpkin.

Chapter Twenty-Two

BACK ON THE BOARD

WHILE ANDREW AND DYLAN ARE DOING THE "GANGNAM STYLE" dance, which I'm shocked is still popular, Sage and I sit on a long board decorated to look like a gangplank on a pirate's ship.

The whole gym looks amazing. There's a half-dozen plastic treasure-chest coolers, some with cold sodas in them, others with ice cream treats. There's even a butcher-paper pirate ship complete with cutout portholes taped to the back wall. It looks almost real if you stand, like, twenty feet away.

I walk over to a chest. "Do you want something cold?" I ask Sage. I open one up. "They have chocolate Drumsticks . . . your favorite."

Sage sighs. "I'm actually trying to be better about

eating junk food," she says. Her eyes wander over to the chest. She shakes her head. "I'll resist and make my mom proud."

"That might be the first time you've ever said no to sugar," I say.

"This is a year of firsts," Sage says. She scoots over so I can sit next to her.

I look out to the dance floor where Ardsley and Tara are performing a synchronized dance. Everyone's watching. They're back in the spotlight, and Sage and I are on the sidelines. I like it this way.

I pull at a tear in my fishnet. "I guess I won't be wearing these to school."

Sage snaps her fingers. I notice that Sage's fingers are healing, and that makes me happy. "Shucks. They'd match our uniform perfectly."

I decide that now is a good time to let her know how much I've missed her.

"I'm really happy that you're here," I say. "I've missed you." I breathe in, trying to prepare myself to ask Sage something that's been bothering me for a long time. "I know the whole piano thing is a sensitive subject, but can I ask you something?"

"Sure," Sage answers.

"Why did you quit?"

Sage takes off her pirate's hat and fiddles with the

string. "If I didn't stop, I would've never had to deal with anything else. When I played four hours a day, it was super-easy to ignore things that I shouldn't ignore. It was like I was playing to get the tough stuff out of my head, but it shouldn't really work that way."

I sigh with relief. I think part of me always worried that it was my fault Sage quit. "So it wasn't completely about your mom's blog? Or my blog?" My stomach feels sick thinking back to the fight Sage and I had in the Everglades.

"Imogene, not everything is about blogging," Sage says, putting her hat back on.

I cover my mouth in fake astonishment. "Just *almost* everything, right?"

"According to our moms, yes," Sage says. "But not to us. I was a little upset with you, because I thought you were pulling away. First you changed the rules of the blog and then you didn't tell me about Dylan or Ardsley."

Even though it pains to hear that I hurt Sage, I'm also happy that she's willing to tell me that I did. That's a sign of a true friendship.

I put my hand on Sage's back. "I'm sorry. I should've realized that I was hurting you. I also should've tried harder to listen to you and figure out what was going on. I didn't mean to abandon you and the Mommy Bloggers' Daughters; I just didn't think it was working anymore."

Sage puts her hand on mine. "It's okay, Imogene. It *wasn't* working. And I was ninety-nine percent mad at my mom and only one percent mad at you. My mom's blog was the thing, and it wasn't the only thing. I felt like my mom wanted to control me—but that she didn't *really* want to know me for real."

I nod. It's so easy to get wrapped up in something— or someone—and forget all about anything else. "I know what you mean. Sometimes I felt like my mom just saw me as Babylicious, not Imogene, and I think I even started to see her only as Mommylicious instead of my mom. It's been much better lately, though."

Sage smiles, and I think how I hope she never changes the gap in her teeth. It's so Sage.

"Things are getting much better between my mom and me too. Who knew that BlogHer, our most dreaded weekend, would end up leading to small miracles? Talking also helped. So did realizing Ed isn't going to take away my mom."

"Ed's the orange farmer?"

Sage holds up her hand. "*Organic* orange farmer. And he's actually okay once you get beyond that goatee."

Sage snaps. "I forgot to tell you that my mom and I are also working on something together. This is the first time we've been on the same page about *anything*. My mom says our chakras are finally aligning—whatever that means."

"What are you guys working on?" I ask.

Sage leans over and whispers in my ear. "It's a secret," she says. "But you can find out if you come to the farmers' market tomorrow."

"I'll be there, then," I whisper back. It reminds me of when Sage and I were little and would play telephone. I watch as Andrew and Dylan make their way toward us.

"Isn't it funny how it seems like nothing happens . . . ," Sage starts.

"And then everything happens," I finish for her.

"That's good," Sage says. "Very bloggable."

"I think I'm done blogging," I say.

Just then Dylan and Andrew make their way to the gangplank.

Dylan points to the dance floor. "You girls do realize that this is a party, right?"

"We might need to make you ladies walk the plank," Andrew adds, high-fiving Dylan.

"I'll be happy to never hear another pirate pun again after tonight," I say.

Sage holds up her index finger. "How about just *one* more?" Sage asks.

"Fine," I say. I hop off the plank.

"Why do pirates have such bad breath?"

I smile because I know the answer. "Because they eat gARRRRlic."

We all laugh even though it's stupid—just like all the other pirate jokes.

I notice Sage tapping on the plank with her fingers, and it gives me a great idea.

I whisper to Dylan when Sage's looking away. "I need your help with something."

He gives me a curious look but nods.

"Be right back, guys," I say. Sage raises her eyebrows, but I just grab Dylan's hand and pull him out of the gym.

"Hold the doors," I tell Dylan.

Dylan does just as I ask. Grandma's right; I really do have good taste.

People think that pianos are heavy, but they're actually pretty easy to move when they are on wheels, like the one from the band room is.

As I wheel the piano into a padded corner of the gym, I get a few looks from some of the teachers. Mr. Anderson starts to walk over toward the piano and me, but Ms. Herring whispers something into his ear and he stops.

Maybe you *do* learn something about someone from reading their blog. I give Ms. Herring a grateful smile. Maybe she actually did know what she was doing with the whole blog project after all, although it certainly caused some drama.

After a minute or two, everyone, including Sage and

Andrew, have turned around and seen the piano in the room. It's like an elephant; it's pretty tough to miss.

I head toward the DJ, who is actually Tara's older brother.

I ask to borrow the microphone and he obliges.

But once I'm holding it, I freeze.

I look at the mob of pirates and my palms start to sweat. Then I look over to Sage. She shrugs and smiles at me. This gives me the courage I need. I tighten my grip so my hands don't slip.

"Hi, everyone," I say, trying to be careful not to talk too close to the microphone. "For one night only, our Sage is coming out of retirement, and she's going to play a song for us tonight. Ninth graders, please give Sage your warm welcome. Because one day, you'll be saying you knew her when."

Everyone claps. Except Sage doesn't budge an inch. I'm worried that I made a huge mistake. But then Andrew whispers something into Sage's ear and gives her a small hug. Then Sage slowly walks over to the piano.

I realize that I'm not everything to Sage anymore, and that's okay. I guess part of growing up is accepting more people into your life—and into your friends' lives.

Dylan stands next to me and nudges me. "Nice one."

Sage sits at the piano and places her fingers above the keys, and it looks like she hasn't been away from it for a single day. In fact, she looks more confident than I've ever seen her before.

Then she starts to play her Philip Glass piece from last year's recital—it's called "Metamorphosis." I know this because Sage talked about it for nearly all of eighth grade. I also had to listen to her practice it more times than I like to remember.

But it sounds amazing. Sage has always been technically good, yet it seems like there's a new life and energy to the way she plays.

But after about thirty seconds, some jerk—I am not sure who—yells out, "Play something you can actually dance to!" Everyone scatters from the dance floor.

My heart thumps and I turn to catch Sage's reaction.

But without missing a beat, Sage transitions into this awesome ballad by Rihanna. Sage is not only playing it perfectly, but she's also smiling. It's the first time I've seen her play the piano and look happy at the same time. It's also the first time I've heard her play a piece that's fun and contemporary.

I look around and people seem impressed with it, but nobody's dancing. Everyone's just watching Sage.

I take my sweaty palm and I grab Dylan's hand. I can't leave Sage out there alone. I lead him to the center of the dance floor. And one by one, guys unglue themselves from the wall and start asking girls to dance.

As we're moving slowly to the music, Dylan whispers, "You know that you owe me another date, right? This one was fun and all, but we spent half of it on Mission Sage."

I lean my head on his shoulder. "Okay. When?"

"Tomorrow," he says.

"Perfect. I even know where we should go," I say. I lead us closer to Sage so I can be one of the first ones to give her a hug after she finishes the Rihanna song.

Tomorrow echoes in my ear.

At the beginning of the year, I thought that every day would always be the same, but change adds up fast. Of course, nothing changes the way you think it will or the way that you try to make it change—but it always does change. Change is the constant.

To: Imogene.luden@internetmail.com
From: grandmalicious@internetmail.com
Subject: <no subject>

hi! im writing my first email ever. going back to
school this old is hard. but I think I'm catching on to
this internet thing. even if I can't figure out how to
capitalize. IS THIS BETTER? I MISS TYPEWRITERS.
I WANTED to say how proud I am of you this year.
I think my Georgia has grown up a lot. I think your
mother has too. (My computer teacher is helping me
now.)

I wanted to give you a piece of advice about life. You
should print this email and hold on to it for when I'm
back on the golf course.

Advice from Grandma Hope: It's really, really easy to
love something—or someone—once. It's much harder
to learn to love something—or someone—the second
time, but it's that second time that usually matters
most. My injury reminded me that we shouldn't limit
ourselves to one love in our life. We should have many
loves, whether that's passions or people. I'm glad
that I'm giving the internet a chance, and I might even
finally accept a date from Fred, that old guy at the
club who keeps pestering me.

Georgia, promise me this: Always be willing to love again. Loving once is easy. Loving twice is harder, but love anytime is always worth it.

Love,

Grandma Hope

PS Let me know that you got this. I still don't trust these things.

To: mommylicious@internetmail.com
From: grandmalicous@internetmail.com
Subject: <no subject>
An old dog can learn new tricks!
I love you, Meg.
And no, I'm not starting a blog.
Mom

The Mommy Bloggers' Daughters: Life with VeggieMom

"Second Chances"

I'm a perfectionist. You have to be in order to be a classical pianist. If one note is wrong, you've messed up the entire piece. Each finger needs to be in a certain place at a certain millisecond. It's not a passion that requires only natural ability; it's a passion that requires relentless perfectionism. It's as much of a science as it is an art.

Maybe I'm too hard on people because I'm a perfectionist. People aren't pianos. You don't hit a certain note and know what you're going to get. I'm sorry, Mom, for not thinking about you and your passions more often. You've always done everything you can to support me and my music.

I know that food and what we eat is

important to you. I know now that we didn't always have food when we wanted it, and often we had to eat food that wasn't good for us—just because it was free or cheap. I understand that you see healthy food as a form of love. I promise that I will keep trying your recipes, and I will try to only sneak fast food once a week . . . okay, once a month.

Thank you, VeggieMom.

Kale and carrots,

VeggieBaby (but only my mom can call me that)

PS Please come check out my mom's and my new venture at the farmers' market on Saturday.

Chapter Twenty-Three

MOTHER OF SAGE

"SO *WHERE* EXACTLY ARE WE GOING, IMOGENE? I THOUGHT I was going to be the mastermind of this date," Dylan says. He's pedaling with his hands at his sides instead of on the handlebars. His black beach cruiser doesn't shake at all.

Inspired, I let one then two hands off my handlebars. I find out that I can also ride without holding on.

"You'll know when we get there." I pedal hard enough that I take the lead. "Follow me, slowpoke," I call out over my shoulder.

It feels good to know that neither my mom nor me is going to post about this date. I won't have to, because I'll remember every tiny detail as long as I live. And the details will be all mine.

Dylan pedals right back up to me. "I want to ride next to you."

"If you put it that way, that's fine." I slow my pace and ride out of the shade and into the sunshine.

We approach a large parking lot near the Third Street shopping area.

"The farmers' market?" Dylan asks.

Every Saturday morning, this parking lot is converted into a farmers' market.

We find a bike rack and lock up our bikes.

"Imogene, I like you and all, but are we already at the 'shopping for groceries' stage?"

I laugh. "Our first date was only last night. We've got—I don't know—a couple of more months before that," I tease.

"You're hysterical," Dylan says as he loops his lock through both our front tires. "Anyone ever tell you that maybe you should start a blog?"

I put my hands on my hips.

"Too soon?" Dylan asks.

I give a laugh and smile to let him know that I'm definitely ready to joke about it—but there's no way I'm starting a new blog any time soon.

I grab his hand and pull him in the direction of the farmers' market.

"Are we looking for organic candles? Homemade baby

clothes? Honey from a local hive?" Dylan asks as we walk through the rows of tables. "McDonald's should start a booth here. They'd make a killing. Everything else here is just so . . . homemade."

He stops in front of Botanicals on the Gulf's booth. He points at the flowers. "Is this why we're here? You want me to buy you flowers? First grocery shopping and now this. I'm not sure my parents are going to be okay with us moving this fast."

Admiring the flowers, I point to the largest bouquet, one made up of pink lilies and orange orchids. "That's the one I want you to buy for me."

Dylan's eyes grow large like giant blue gumballs. "Seriously?"

"Of course not," I say, and I pull him away from the table.

Dylan fake-wipes his forehead. "Phew," he says. "I was going to have to get a job. My parents definitely don't pay me that well for taking out the trash."

Up ahead, Sage waves at me from her table. She nudges Ms. Carter, who sees us and also waves.

"Oh, I see now," Dylan says. "You brought me to show off to your BFF."

"Nope," I say. "I'm bringing *you* to my BFF to show off how awesome *she* is."

We make our way through the small crowd that's

gathered in front of Sage and her mom. They're both wearing green aprons and Sage's curly hair is pulled back in a thick braid. On their table, there are a few small mason jars filled with different types of jams, each a different color. Taped above the table is an awesome banner that reads MOTHER OF SAGE. It's written in a green font that looks like vines.

"This *so* genius," I say, and smile at Sage. "I guess playing the piano's not your only talent."

Sage pulls her braid over her shoulder. "Thanks," she says. "I even convinced my mom that we could add a dash of sugar to each jar. We met in the middle for once."

Ms. Carter laughs and points toward herself. "Actually, I think *I* did most of the compromising. I didn't want *any* sugar *and* I told you that I'd focus on Mother of Sage, not my blog."

I raise my eyebrows and Sage smiles from ear to ear. I guess change is all around.

I pick up a jar filled with key lime jelly. The label design matches the banner and looks adorable. "How are sales so far today?"

Sage looks up from her accounting book and picks up a jar. "That's our last key lime! We've already broken even, including the banner and rental spot at the market. Pretty stellar for our first day."

I look around and point at the remaining jars. "It seems like everyone here is packing up their booths for the day. How about this: I'll buy the rest of the jars, and then let's all go to the beach. Before we know it, Naples is going to be bombarded with tourists. Let's take advantage of the day."

"You've got a deal," she says.

Sage pulls out a simple brown paper bag stamped with the Mother of Sage logo and starts filling it with jams.

Dylan shrugs. "But what can I buy?" he asks, looking at the nearly empty table.

"You'll have to place a special order or come back next Saturday," Sage says seriously.

When Dylan takes off to find a restroom and some fried food, Sage gives her mom a look until finally Ms. Carter announces that she's going to make a trip to the car.

The second they're both out of earshot, I let out a shriek. "Ohmigosh, Sage. This year is turning out to be all right. We're figuring things out with our moms. You have this awesome business. You and Andrew are adorable. I'm on a date with Dylan. We're having a *total* time."

Sage looks around. "It *has* somehow turned out okay. It took us a while, but I like where we are now."

I hand over my allowance to Sage. "And with each jar,

you're that much closer to Juilliard, if, of course, that's what you decide you want to do."

Sage mimics punching numbers into a calculator. "Actually, we'd have to sell about a half a million jars to pay for Juilliard. I did the stats last night, so maybe I'm still interested in applying there," Sage says with a wink. "But I also read that they have a lot of scholarships available. So who knows? And, Imogene, it looks like you're a half of a date away from being Dylan's girlfriend."

I've been my parents' child, Sage's best friend, the star of Mommylicious, and the author of a blog, but I've never been anyone's *girlfriend*. I like the way that sounds.

"Shh. I see Dylan walking back over," I whisper. Even though I'm really hoping this works out, I definitely don't want him thinking that I'm planning our future children's names. (I already did that back in eighth grade. Ophelia and Lawson.)

Sage starts cleaning up the table, but then she pauses. "Imogene, thank you for last night. Really. I'm happy that you made me play. Once I feel like the other problems with my mom are sorted out, I'm definitely going to start practicing again. Maybe I will even get into Juilliard. Thank you for reminding me how much I love it. I think I can actually hear the music better without everything else that was in my head. Seriously."

"I know what you mean," I say as I help Sage clean the table. Since my mom and I talked, I've been able to see beyond her blog—beyond her being Mommylicious.

When Dylan approaches the table, he pulls out two daisies from behind his back.

"One for each of the Mommy Bloggers' Daughters," Dylan says. "Or are you all the Former Mommy Bloggers' Daughters?"

Sage gives me an "Is this guy for real?" look. We both take the flowers and tuck them behind our ears.

"And if you could, like, not Facebook, Tweet, or blog that I just did that, that would be greatly appreciated. I need to be able to go to school on Monday without being tormented by my friends."

"Thank you, Dylan," I say. I don't care if I'm blushing the same color as a peony.

Ms. Carter comes back into the booth just as we promise not to post anything about it online. "Sage, can we get just one photo of us at our booth?"

Sage rolls her eyes. "That didn't take long," she says. "Once a blogger, always a blogger."

"I want it for our Christmas card," Ms. Carter says and rolls her own eyes. "Have a little faith in me."

Sage hands me her mom's cell phone. "One picture," she consents. "That's it."

They smile, and luckily, the first shot is perfect.

Right after I hand back the phone, Ms. Carter says, "You know, it might make a great homepage picture for our website. Just saying."

"See what I said," Sage says. Then she gives her mom a hug.

"Beach time?" I ask.

"Beach time."

The Blog Once Known as Mommylicious

Now MegLuden.Com

As you all have read recently, this has been a tough year, both as a mom and as Mommylicious. What I initially thought were silly, hormonal protests by my daughter to stop blogging about her turned out to be genuine requests for privacy. I understand now where she's coming from.

I'll admit that through the blog, I was trying to freeze-frame time. While the blog started out as a way to document Imogene growing up, I see now that it became my way of trying to keep her young forever. If I kept writing about Babylicious, she'd still grow up, but she'd resent me for trying to keep her under my thumb and microscope. I've learned that growing up isn't only for kids . . . and sometimes it requires a healthy dose of letting go.

Although a great part of my life (and a source of great happiness) has been being Mommylicious, my role as a mother offline is what's most impor- tant to me. With a heavy heart, I'm shutting down MommyliciousMeg.com. To my faithful readers and sponsors, thank you for an amazing fifteen years. You are all in my thoughts and prayers.

In happier news, I'm starting a new blog. Before I was a blogger, I had always wanted to be a writer of fiction. Motherhood—and this blog—sidetracked me from this goal, but I've just completed my application to a Master of Fine Arts program for creative writing to get back into it. I'm hoping I'll take all the lessons I learned about life and love from the blog and use them for the stories that have always danced around in the back of my head.

Also, I'll be spending more time with my family— offline. I've been to the beach only three times in the last 365 days . . . *and* I live in Florida . . . *and* I spent the entire time blogging about it. Imogene has showed me that sometimes you have to disconnect to reconnect, so I'm unplugging and heading to the beach.

Please STAY IN TOUCH and if you'd like, please read MY BLOG about trying to become a writer. I can't promise that I'll blog every day. But I do promise that when I do blog, I'll really have something to say—and that it'll be about only me.

Thanks for all the years.

Love Always,

Mommylicious

The Mommy Bloggers' Daughters:
The Girl on That Blog

"Don't Dare Call Me Babylicious . . .
Signing Off"

Every other day, there's a news piece about kids being so connected to the internet that they're disconnected from everywhere else. There are even videos of babies trying to swipe actual magazine pages like they would do on an iPad screen. We're living in a crazy world, one where we're never completely in the minute because we're so attached and wrapped up with our technology.

As I can well tell you, it's *easy* to get your online identity mixed up with your real identity.

And it's *easy* to hide behind a computer and say things that you're too afraid to say in real life, or things that you shouldn't be saying at all—online or offline.

And it's *easy* to get caught up with

people paying attention to you because of something that's online about you.

And it's *easy* just to point fingers and say that the internet is destroying our culture.

But *we are* the internet. We can choose to use it either to connect or disconnect from one another and from ourselves.

From now on, I'm going to focus on my real-life connections. I'll still continue blogging for English class, but I'll be keeping it simple—and private. Maybe one day, I will have another personal public blog, but I seriously doubt it.

Yours Truly,

Imogene

PS Check out my mom's new blog: www.MegLuden.com.

PPS My friend Ardsley has some great fashion advice on her blog. Warm-weather readers, if you want to find out how to stay cool and stay stylish, go here:

www.mermaidsmanicuresandmacaroons.com.

ACKNOWLEDGMENTS

FIRST AND FOREMOST, THANK YOU TO MY READERS. I WRITE FOR you all. Please contact me at gwendolyn.heasley@gmail.com with any feedback. I love hearing from readers, and your energy and support keeps me writing.

To Sarah Dotts Barley, my editor, I'm in your debt forever. Your intellect and wisdom made this book so much stronger. Thank you.

To everyone who worked on *Don't Call Me Baby* at HarperTeen, this book is also yours. This book only exists because of your team efforts and collaboration. I appreciate everything that you all did in order to get this book into readers' hands.

To my agent, Leigh Feldman, and her assistant, Jean Garnett, thank you for being both my sounding boards and my advocates. Your dedication and hard work allow me to focus on the other stuff, and I'm so thankful to you both.

To Sarah Burningham, my publicist, you continue to be my Little Bird. Thank you for helping get my characters and words out into the world.

To my friends, being an author can be lonely, but I'm lucky to have The. Best. Friends. In. The. World. Your friendship keeps me company even when I'm alone at my writing desk.

To Vermont College of Fine Arts, particularly the Magic Ifs, thank you, and YAM!

To my in-laws, sisters-in-law, and their husbands, I'm so lucky to count you all as family.

To my parents and my sister, Aliceyn, I couldn't do anything without your outstanding and unfailing support and love. My accomplishments are also yours. You can't choose your family, but I would choose you all if I could. Enmeshment is in.

To Cory and Cricket, my husband and baby girl, I love you. 2013 was totally our year! I must have been born under some lucky stars. . . . Here's to many more wonderful years.

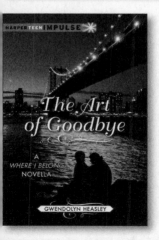